"You mea[illegible]
Cressida [illegible]

"Oh, no . . . you m[illegible]" Sir Piers came around to stand beside her, riffling through the pages on the desk. "What I meant was, I should have helped you, not let you take all the responsibility. From what I can see, it looks fine—very good, in fact."

"Thank you, Sir Piers." Cressida's shoulders relaxed with relief.

Then, so quietly she wasn't sure she'd heard correctly, he said, "I think it's time we dropped the 'Sir.' "

"Piers?" All the emotions she'd been suppressing swept over her like a tidal wave as he drew her close.

Then, slowly, gently, his lips sought hers. She felt his arms slide around her, and with a gasp she fell against him. This proud, reclusive man, who'd been so remote, was actually holding her in his arms!

HEART OF MARBLE

Helena Dawson

Harlequin Books

TORONTO • NEW YORK • LONDON
AMSTERDAM • PARIS • SYDNEY • HAMBURG
STOCKHOLM • ATHENS • TOKYO • MILAN

Original hardcover edition published in 1989
by Mills & Boon Limited

ISBN 0-373-03008-8

Harlequin Romance first edition October 1989

Printed in U.S.A.

CHAPTER ONE

'ARE you quite sure you'll be all right?' Dr Heaton looked up at his daughter anxiously, a protective frown creasing his forehead. 'I don't like leaving you here, Cressida. I've never seen such a forlorn-looking place —and there's no sign of life anywhere.'

Worriedly he looked round, then peered at his watch.

'I must be off soon, too . . . I'm due at the hospital at six.'

Cressida leant her arm on the top of the car and bent down to kiss the top of her father's head.

'I'll be fine, Dad, honest. I'm sure Sir Piers must be around somewhere. He's probably been called away. Or he's forgotten when I said I'd be arriving. I told you he was old and absent-minded!'

'There must be someone else around, surely? What about his wife . . . Is he married, do you know? Ring the bell again. I want to see everything's in order before I leave.'

Cressida straightened up and stared down at her father with mock severity in her green eyes.

'I'm twenty-five, Dad. I'm a big girl now, and quite able to look after myself. You get back to your patients, and I'll wait around here till someone puts in an appearance. Somebody's bound to come sooner or later—look, they'd hardly have left the windows open if they were all going to be out.'

Dr Heaton glanced up at the mullioned windows with a disapproving sniff. 'It doesn't look as though they've been cleaned for centuries—you can see the dust from here.'

Cressida grinned. 'You can't expect an Elizabethan manor house to come up to hospital standards of cleanliness . . . oh, go on, Dad. I'll phone you if there's a hitch. If I'm stranded, I can always spend the night in that nice pub in the village where we had lunch.'

Dr Heaton's hand hovered uncertainly over the steering wheel.

'You'll let us know how you get on—come home if there's any problem?'

'I'll let you know, I promise. And there won't be any problems, I'm sure. Sir Piers was quite specific in his letter about what the job entailed—he didn't seem *that* vague.'

She stooped and kissed her father again. 'Thanks for bringing me, Dad—and don't worry! Go on, off with you and let me go and find my boss.'

Dr Heaton opened his mouth to speak, then thought better of it and gave his daughter a rueful smile again. As she had said, she was quite old enough to look after herself . . . he was worrying unnecessarily. And, if it didn't work out, Suffolk wasn't exactly at the ends of the earth. She could easily give up the job and come home to Kent.

He turned the ignition and put the car into gear. 'Good luck, then, Cress—I hope it all works out. Let us know when you expect to open—your mother and I want to be the first visitors.'

'I'll hold you to that,' Cressida told him, smiling, 'but I'll be in touch before that—maybe even come home for the odd weekend.'

She watched her father as he turned the car in the paved courtyard, and set off down the long drive, finally vanishing through the great iron gates.

She was alone; she stared round uncertainly—her father had been quite right. There was no sign of life anywhere, not even the bark of a dog to greet her. In spite of her brave words, a sharp twinge of loneliness threatened to overcome her earlier optimism as she stood with her pile of luggage in front of the great main doorway of Clarewood Priory.

Like two arms, the wings of the building stretched out on either side, but with no welcoming warmth in the gesture. The iron-studded wooden doors facing her looked firmly closed against all intruders. Like its owner, the house seemed to be holding itself aloof.

There was a stone bench on the far side of the courtyard, and Cressida made her way towards it, almost feeling she should tiptoe in the enveloping silence. She settled herself in the sun to absorb the atmosphere and wait for somebody to appear, for not even the sound of her father's departing car had been enough to rouse any interest.

In spite of the dust disapproved of by her father, the leaded windows sparkled faintly in the pale April sunlight which also warmed the mellow brick of the walls. For all its air of privacy, it was an attractive house, and not too imposing in spite of its great age. She knew it had been built in the grounds of a priory . . . Cressida fished in her bag and brought out the notes she had made when she was preparing for a possible interview with Sir Piers Aylward as soon as she had applied for the job here. But reading about a place, even a historic house like this, wasn't at all the same as seeing it for yourself—and that, of course, was precisely what she was going to try to persuade people to discover.

It had been quite by chance that Cressida had seen the advertisement in one of the magazines in her father's surgery.

'No wonder you're the most popular doctor for miles around,' she would tease him. 'It's not the bedside manner which gets the patients queueing up—just the brand new mags you put in your surgery.'

She had been feeling restless in her present job for some time. Being a secretary in an estate agent in the small market town where her father had his practice scarcely offered the challenge she felt she needed to give her scope to exercise the talent for organisation she had discovered when she had taken over the running of her mother's antiques market during a family crisis. The knowledge she had picked up at that time would stand her in good stead now—at least, she hoped so. Maybe she *had* bitten off more than she could chew, but she was always one to act impulsively and think afterwards, and when she had seen the ad. for the job of organising the opening up of Clarewood Priory to the public, she had decided to take the plunge and apply.

'I don't suppose there's any chance I'll get the job,' she had told her parents, 'but there's no harm in trying, is there? And I might get a nice trip to Suffolk for an interview with . . . who is it?' She'd peered at the paper. 'Sir Piers Aylward.' She'd frowned thoughtfully. 'Now, there's a good historical-sounding name . . . I see him as tall, elderly and rather absent-minded, in a very gentlemanly sort of way. All shabby tweeds—well cut, of course—with a spaniel . . . oh, and a pipe.'

Her mother had laughed. 'You always did let your imagination run away with you—hadn't you better wait till you meet him before you get quite carried away?'

But she never did get to meet Sir Piers. She had taken endless trouble with her application, knowing her lack of relevant experience might—probably would—put her at a disadvantage if there was a lot of competition for the job. She had tried to compensate by making her covering letter as interesting and enthusiastic as she could, and maybe that was what had appealed to her future employer . . . . 'Or else no one else applied,' Cressida had said gloomily. 'Maybe there's something wrong with the place, or with the owner, that everybody knows about except me.'

For Sir Piers had offered her the job almost by return of post—there was no question of an interview. All the arrangements had been made by letter, perfectly businesslike and efficient, but completely impersonal.

'Dear Miss Heaton,' he had written. 'I have read your curriculum vitae and taken note of your qualifications. If it is convenient to you, I should be glad if you could come and take up your position here at the end of April.

'You will, of course, be given accommodation in the Priory, and the salary will be . . .' He had named the sum which was respectable, if not generous, and after a few qualms Cressida decided to accept.

'It's funny, though, that he didn't want to see me,' she had commented. 'As I'm actually going to be living there, you'd think he would want to meet me before making his mind up.'

Her mother had frowned. 'I hope it's all above board. I suppose it's all right to let you stay there.'

Cressida gave a peal of laughter and gave her mother an affectionate hug.

'You dear, old-fashioned thing—of course I'll be all right. I'm a big, strong girl now, and quite able to look after myself.' She drew herself up to her full five feet, eight inches and tossed back her dark hair, flexing her muscles.

'I'm more than a match for any weedy old aristocrat, and if it's white slave traffic he's into . . .'

'You'll probably organise that for him, too.'

They had both laughed and her mother had given up. 'Well, just remember we're here if you need us . . . or if it doesn't work out.'

And now, here she was, about to start work for a man she still hadn't met—her heart gave a little flutter of apprehension. Maybe she should have volunteered to come and introduce herself first, but until now she hadn't considered it necessary. She had never had any difficulty in getting on with people.

A gust of wind flicked at the corner of the papers she was holding, heralding the appearance of a large cloud which blotted out the sun, and shook Cressida from her reverie. She shivered in the sudden chill, and somewhere in the distance a clock struck.

She had been left waiting here for an hour—this was ridiculous! Her mood changed from one of polite tolerance to irritation. How dared they leave her here like this? It was too bad, and very rude. Titled or not, no man had any right to keep a girl—whether employee or guest—waiting around unwelcomed. The time had come to take matters into her own hands.

Leaving her luggage in the middle of the courtyard, Cressida strode resolutely back to the great wooden door. She had already tried the bell once, and now she leant on it again, hard, listening for the answering peal. But there was no sound. Either it rang somewhere out of earshot, or else it was broken.

Maybe the handle? Cautiously Cressida grasped the big iron ring and gave it a tentative twist. It slipped round easily under her fingers, and she pushed the door gently. To her surprise it opened . . . well, they'd asked for it. She would let herself in and wait inside.

It was like stepping into another age. The door opened straight into a long, high-ceilinged room, stone-flagged and panelled with carved oak. Cressida gasped, simultaneously drawing her jacket round her with an instinctive gesture against the cold. What a room! At least, no, not a room—that was far too domestic a word for something so grand. This must be the Great Hall.

A huge fireplace heaped with logs faced her, and a long table ran the length of the hall, with heavy wooden benches set on either side as though waiting still for the household to take their places for dinner. A smaller table and carved chairs were placed on a low dais for the master and his family.

The effect was stark and sombre. The only light came from narrow, leaded windows set high in one wall, the only decoration the heavy oak carving and intricately moulded plasterwork on the ceiling.

But what caught the eye most of all were the portraits. The forbidding chill which had immediately oppressed Cressida on her entrance came not only from the stone floor and empty fireplace, but from the stern gaze of past generations of Aylwards staring down at this unbidden visitor who had come to disturb their peace. And not a smile among them.

Cressida walked slowly round from one Aylward to another. Some of them were in uniform, the length of hair varied according to the fashion of the age, one or two even sported beards, but there were definite family characteristics she began to recognise as she proceeded from the early Tudor ancestors through the centuries to what was clearly the latest addition to the gallery. This last Alyward, with his stern mouth and steely gaze, bore little resemblance to the elderly, tweedy gentleman of her imagination. Who was he? Not her Sir Piers, surely—or so she hoped. His father, maybe . . . Cressida moved closer to get a better look.

Then the slightest of sounds behind her made her swing round—she felt the colour drain from her cheeks as her heart seemed to leap into her throat. She was no longer alone. The figure of a man had materialised through the wall opposite where there was no door, and was standing, motionless, observing her silently with that same icy appraisal mirrored in the portraits. It was as though one of them had come to ghostly life.

Cressida's breath came in gasps and she leant against the wall for support, mesmerised by the apparition in the corner.

'Miss Heaton?'

The voice was as cold as his eyes. Cressida nodded, not daring to trust her voice. He walked slowly towards her, his rubber-soled shoes making no sound on the stone flags . . . of course he wasn't a ghost, that was silly, but the silence of his approach, the concentrated stare, all added to the illusion. But where had he come from?

Cressida glanced past him to the spot where he had first appeared. She couldn't see a door, yet common sense told her there must be one.

The faintest shadow of a smile momentarily curved the stern mouth.

'There's a door in the panelling,' he said in brief explanation. 'I am sorry if I startled you.'

Cressida grinned ruefully and stepped forward. So he *was* human, and he must, surely, be her employer, Sir Piers Aylward. Certainly an Aylward, anyway—she would recognise those straight, dark brows over the steely eyes anywhere now, and the defiant chin which seemed to invite challenge. The likeness to the portraits surrounding them was startling, but not quite a carbon copy. Something about the high forehead and curve of the cheekbones was not typical . . . inherited from his mother's side, perhaps? And how had he got that tan?

'When you've quite finished, Miss Heaton . . .?'

Cressida flushed, then gave an apologetic laugh.

'That was very rude of me—I'm sorry. You must get tired of people telling you how alike you all are . . .' She waved a hand towards the portraits. 'I was studying them while I was waiting. You are Sir Piers—Sir Piers Aylward?'

His distinctive features left her in no real doubt, but those faded cords and shabby Aran sweater hardly added up to her image of a baronet from an old and distinguished family. And what about her elderly, pipe-smoking tweedy gentleman? This man couldn't be more than about thirty-five at the most.

Gravely he inclined his head and held out his hand. Cressida took it in hers and a tremor, unexpected in its strength and suddenness, ran up her arm. The firm grasp was warm and quite at odds with the coolness of his expression. Startled, she raised her eyes to his, but to her disappointment she read no answering response on his face, and the moment passed. Still, she thought, with a lift of the heart, it did show that somewhere beneath that severe exterior real human feelings must exist. She waited demurely for him to speak.

Sir Piers hesitated a moment, as though uncertain of what to do next, and he ran his long, brown fingers through his hair with a frown.

'You have some luggage?'

Cressida nodded. 'It's out in the courtyard. My father brought me, but he had to leave. He's a doctor, you see, and had to get back to the hospital—and then we couldn't make anyone hear, so after waiting outside for a while I tried the door, and came in here to wait . . .'

She ran out of steam, sensing that she was irritating Sir Piers by her chatter. He was obviously a man of few words, and if they were to work together she would have to try to curb her tendency to what her parents called 'chuntering on'.

'Shall I go and get my cases?' she enquired cheerfully. 'And perhaps you could ask someone to show me where I should put them—then I can get settled in before we get down to business.'

Sir Piers gave a short laugh. 'I hope you didn't come here under the impression that I had a large staff to run the house and wait on you hand and foot, Miss Heaton? I have some part-time help—Mrs Bryant comes in from the village most mornings, but there's no one else.'

He swung on his heel and headed towards the main door. 'Come with me and I'll show you your room.'

Cressida followed him, trying her best to repress the irritation which was threatening to boil over. Not only had he not apologised for keeping her waiting so long, but she had hardly been made to feel welcome when Sir Piers had finally condescended to arrive—and now, to crown it all, he had as good as accused her of being a class-conscious snob, or something very like it.

Of course she didn't expect to be waited on—what did he take her for? She was sorely tempted to make some kind of retort in self-defence. The sooner he realised what kind of girl she was, the better . . . but, as she caught up with him by the door, she changed her mind. This wasn't the moment—there would be plenty of opportunity to speak her mind when—if—she got to know him better.

Sir Piers opened the door and stood back to let her go through first. As she went past him, Cressida's shoulder brushed against his outstretched arm. She turned to smile at him and was astonished to see him start back as though he had been stung, with an expression almost of alarm. But she had barely touched him! She hesitated for a moment, but what could she say? She went on out into the daylight as though nothing had happened, but filed the strange occurrence away in her mind for future reference.

Sir Piers closed the door behind her and strode past towards the pile of luggage untidily cluttering up the forecourt of his house. Silhouetted against the open sky, she could see him better now than in the dim light of the Great Hall.

He was a lot broader than she had thought, the strong muscles of his shoulders showing beneath the shapeless pullover, and he walked with an unconscious grace and lightness of step that hinted at a latent athleticism. Cressida got the definite impression, watching him, that here was someone who had lived a lot of his time in the open air—and that deep tan hadn't come just from pottering round the estate, nor from a fortnight's skiing.

The fitful April sun had emerged from the clouds again and struck silvery glints from the straight fair hair which fell forward as he bent to pick up the suitcases. Cressida hurried forward to help him—it didn't seem right that her employer should do all the donkey-work—but he swung her assortment of bags and cases up as though they were no heavier than a few light parcels, the muscles of his thighs tightening as he straightened up with a heavy case grasped in each brown hand.

'This way,' he said curtly, and set off towards the right-hand wing of the building with not so much as a backward look to check that Cressida was following.

Did he never make conversation? She was in for a lonely time unless she could somehow break down that barrier of reserve.

Sir Piers stopped outside a low door set in the brick wall.

'Would you mind opening it?' he asked. 'And bend your head as you go through. Some of these doorways are rather low—my ancestors were clearly shorter than we are.'

Cressida hurried forward to do what he asked, cheered by a small spurt of satisfaction at this quite lengthy speech and one which told her he had at least noticed her above-average height. It wasn't much, but it was a start.

She waited until he had passed through, then closed the door behind him. They were in what must have been the workshop and storage area of the original manor, disused now, the empty rooms opening off a whitewashed passageway which ran the length of the wing.

'In there.' Sir Piers nodded to a door adjacent to the archway leading back to the main house, and Cressida found herself in a light, airy room furnished almost spartanly with an old, battered desk and chair, two ancient armchairs which even her relatively untutored eye told her dated probably at least back to the eighteenth century, a filing cabinet, also scratched and battered, and an old electric fire. And that was all.

'This is your office,' Sir Piers told her—so he did know why she was here! She was beginning to wonder, since so far he hadn't even mentioned her supposed job. And where was she to sleep?

'Your bedroom is through there.' Sir Piers indicated yet another door leading out of the 'office'. Cressida walked across and peered through into a small room even more spartan—or simple, if you wanted to be polite—than the other. It contained a bed, a wash-basin recently fitted, if the label still adhering to the cold tap was anything to go by, a wardrobe, a chest of drawers and a hard, upright chair. Nothing else, not even a bed-side-lamp. It looked like a boarding school of a particularly puritanical kind.

Sir Piers put her cases down on the office floor and

made no attempt to come any further.

Does he think he's going to be compromised if he comes into a girl's bedroom? Cressida wondered in amusement. Judging from the episode by the main door only a few minutes ago, she wouldn't be at all surprised. Or maybe Lady Aylward, wherever she is, is a particularly jealous woman. That at least would explain his alarmed reaction to any physical contact. She would have to wait and find out.

'This is fine,' she told him, thinking privately it was a good job these cases contained several of her cherished possessions from home. The Welsh rugs and collection of ornaments would do a little to brighten up the rooms. It was amazing how soon you could make your own imprint on even the most discouraging surroundings.

Sir Piers was standing at the office window, gazing out at the gardens beyond, his back towards her. She dared not join him for fear of frightening him away, but stood in the centre of the room watching him unobserved.

His brown hands were linked tightly behind his back but his forefingers beat a little rhythmic tattoo against one another. Cressida cleared her throat—his nervousness was catching.

'What would you like me to do, Sir Piers? Unpack and get organised here, then discuss exactly what you have in mind for me . . . for my work?' she corrected herself hurriedly, seeing the double-entendre an over-sensitive man might suspect.

He turned round to face her, and Cressida was again struck by the suppressed strength and power that lay concealed beneath that over-controlled exterior.

'I'll show you where to find me when you're ready, Miss Heaton.' The level gaze met hers, then, as though relieved to be on the move, Sir Piers crossed the room to the door and pointed to the archway.

'My study is just through there on the left—and there's a cloakroom too, a little way beyond it.' Again that frosty glimmer of a smile. 'I'm sorry this house isn't as well equipped with modern conveniences as it might be, but the cloakroom doubles as a shower-room which you are welcome to use whenever you wish.'

'Thank you very much,' Cressida replied, 'and whatever you might think—I'm sorry if I gave you the wrong impression—I didn't really expect to be living in the lap of luxury.'

As soon as she had spoken, she began to have misgivings. She could have phrased that better. This man seemed to have the knack of making her say all the wrong things. She directed a surreptitious glance in his direction, but he appeared not to have noticed as he stood restlessly examining the stonework in the passage with an anxious frown.

'I'll go and unpack, then,' Cressida offered, 'and come and find you as soon as I've organised myself.'

He said nothing, but gave a quick nod before disappearing into the main part of the house, leaving Cressida alone once again.

CHAPTER TWO

CRESSIDA worked quickly, putting her clothes away in the cupboard and chest and leaving the arranging of her other possessions until later.

She stood in the silent room that was to be her office, trying to visualise it as a bustling hive of activity, noisy with the sound of telephones and typewriter—but this time her imagination failed her and a feeling of helplessness threatened to overcome her naturally optimistic spirits.

Not for the first time, she began to wonder what she was doing here, and how she was going to co-exist with the strange, withdrawn man who was her employer. For a wild moment she almost felt tempted to shovel all her things back into the suitcases and make her escape back to the busy world outside the Priory gates where people enjoyed making conversation and didn't mind brushing against one another in the course of ordinary, everyday living. Maybe she should take up lodgings in that nice village pub—she remembered the open, pleasant features of the landlord and his outgoing wife. She could always borrow a bike and come in from there . . .

The slam of a door somewhere in the house roused her from her reflections. She had come here to do a job, and she hadn't even begun yet. She must at least give it—and him—a chance before turning tail and running away. Sir Piers might mellow once he got to know her better.

She went back into the bedroom and stooped to peer

at herself in the small mirror on the chest of drawers. Solemn green eyes stared back at her as she dabbed some powder on her nose—tip-tilted, not nobly straight like those of the Aylward ancestors—and touched up the rosy lipstick on her wide mouth.

Not a face to launch a thousand ships, she thought ruefully, not even a small canoe—but then, why should she worry? She doubted whether Sir Piers would notice if she were Elizabeth Taylor's double.

'Oh, well, best go and see what's what,' she told her reflection out loud, deriving a modicum of comfort from the sound of a human voice, even though it was only her own. She brushed down the sensible grey flannel skirt she had thought suitable for the job of administrator, flicked back her dark hair and went back into the passage, listening. There wasn't a sound.

Again she was uncomfortably aware of the sound her heels made on the flagstones as she made her way through the archway and into the main part of the house. It was as though she were disturbing the peace of centuries.

She found the study just to the left of the hall. Sir Piers had left the door open and as she stood, hesitating on the threshold, she took the opportunity to examine her surroundings.

The room gave a much more comfortable impression than either the Great Hall or her quarters. It looked really lived-in with its leather armchairs and faded Persian rugs on the wood-block floor. The high, oak-panelled walls were lined with books from floor to ceiling, and a quick glance told Cressida they were not the sort of books you saw in most stately homes, rows of neatly matched leather volumes more for show than study. These were real books, read and used by someone who had collected them together for a purpose.

Sir Piers gave no sign that he was aware of her presence. He stood by the window, broad shoulders tensely hunched and hands agitating nervously behind his back. He reminded Cressida of some wild animal who had strayed into an unfamiliar habitat and was longing to find its way home again.

She cleared her throat and he spun round.

'I'm sorry,' Cressida apologised. 'I didn't mean to make you jump—I thought you must have heard me.'

She walked forward to the chair Sir Piers was indicating by the wide desk which lay between them—a desk so immaculately tidy that Cressida was reminded of one of the favourite sayings of her old headmistress: 'Always remember, girls, a tidy desk is the sign of a tidy mind!' Well, Miss Marshall would have been proud of Sir Piers—his mind must be an object lesson in orderliness. There was hardly anything on the desk-top at all, except for a couple of folders and a tray of pens and pencils.

Cressida sat down and folded her hands on her lap, waiting expectantly for him to speak. The penetrating grey eyes under the distinctive Aylward brows stared uncertainly at her for a moment, then he gave a little sigh.

'You're settled in, Miss Heaton? You have enough space for your things?'

'Oh, yes, thanks,' Cressida said cheerfully. 'And I'll soon have the rooms looking quite homely with all the bits and pieces I've brought with me.'

Sir Piers nodded and drew a folder towards him, placing it squarely in front of him. 'If there's anything you need, tell me, please . . . this situation is something quite unfamiliar to me.' He frowned again as he perused the papers in the folder.

For goodness' sake, Cressida thought, exasperated,

why doesn't he get on with it? It was all she could do not to leap up and seize the file from him, to galvanise him into some sort of action. If one of them didn't take the initiative, they would be here for ever!

'What exactly do you want me to do, Sir Piers?' Cressida drew her chair in to the desk and leant forward. 'Shall I make some notes—when do you plan on opening up the house, for example?'

The cool eyes lifted to meet hers dispassionately. 'There's one thing I must tell you before we discuss anything else, Miss Heaton, and that is that, once you have begun organising this scheme, I do not wish to be bothered by any of the details. And I mean *any* of them,' he repeated firmly. 'I have my own preoccupations—I am employing you to take complete charge.'

He rose and went back again to his favourite position by the window as though he longed to be out in the fresh air and not cooped up inside discussing disagreeable plans in which he had clearly little or no interest.

'I see.' Cressida spoke slowly, taken aback by this unexpected revelation. She thought quickly. 'In that case, hadn't I better know exactly what you want me to do— which rooms are to be on show, how much I can spend on advertising and so on? There's a lot to be decided and I can't do that on my own.'

Sir Piers turned back to face her, a slight smile hovering at the corner of his lips. The effect was startling—like the sun appearing on a winter's day, Cressida thought fancifully.

'You're not frightened by the responsibility?'

Cressida met his questioning look full on. 'I must admit I'm a little surprised. I'd have thought . . .' She broke off as the winter sun disappeared abruptly behind the now familiar cloud. 'But not frightened,' she went on firmly. 'Once I know what's expected, I'm sure I can manage. At least, I'll have a good try.'

Sir Piers' relief at Cressida's positive response was

obvious, and his expression softened into lines less forbidding than those in which it had been set up until now. Cressida began to feel quite cheered—at least she knew he *could* begin to relax . . .

But she might have known it was too good to last. Back came the clouds again as his jaw tightened at some further unwelcome thought.

'I'd better tell you why I need you here at all,' he began.

'I imagined you just wanted to open Clarewood Priory to the public?' Cressida ventured. 'To let people see what a lovely place you have.'

Sir Piers' eyes flashed. 'Clarewood Priory has been a private home since the 1580s and, if I had my way, that is what it would have remained. You don't think I *want* people tramping round, making stupid comments and leaving their dirty fingermarks all over the walls and furniture, do you?'

Cressida was taken aback. 'Then why . . .'

'Because if I don't raise money this way, and in any other way I can, I shall have to sell it.' The voice was harsh and his brown fingers clenched fiercely at his sides before he moved swiftly back to his chair and sat down facing Cressida, his face pale under the tan.

'I'm sorry—I had no idea,' Cressida said softly.

'Of course you hadn't—it's not something I wish broadcast about, the fact that I find myself almost bankrupt. It isn't—wasn't—anybody's business except mine, or at least it wouldn't have been if I hadn't had to find someone to help me save the house . . . my family home.'

Cressida wondered why, if the Priory meant so much to him, he hadn't taken on the job himself, but she knew better than to interrupt. As if he had read her thoughts, Sir Piers continued, 'There are two reasons why I needed someone else to organise the visitors idea. The first is simple——' Again that fugitive hint of a smile. 'You may have noticed, Miss Heaton, that I am not altogether at ease with strangers . . .?'

Cressida didn't know what to say, however much she wanted to agree with him, but she was saved the embarrassment of finding a suitable reply as he went on, 'You don't need to answer that—but I know my limitations, and I am well aware that I would not be the ideal person to be in charge of public relations. The second reason . . .' He frowned, then got to his feet again, but this time, instead of going to the window, he moved over to the door. 'I'll show you over the house and try to explain how it is that I'm in the situation I described a moment ago.'

As he held the door open, Cressida made quite sure this time that she came nowhere near him. She was beginning to have just the faintest glimmer of understanding of what made this strange man tick, and realised how repugnant any kind of physical contact was to him. She would have to be careful—her instinct was always to touch people, put her hand on an arm, kiss a cheek without its having any special significance. But Sir Piers, she knew already, would find any such gesture abhorrent.

'I don't know how much you know about the Priory?' Sir Piers asked her, leading the way back towards the Great Hall. 'We'll start from here, as this is the oldest part of the building and where you'll probably want the tour to start.'

'You think guided tours, rather than letting people come and go as they please?'

They were standing beneath the portrait of a man who Sir Piers told her was Sir Roger, the Aylward who had been responsible for the building of the Priory.

Cressida could almost feel the disapproval emanating from that stern face so like that of the man by her side. He wouldn't have wanted tourists invading the privacy of his home any more than did his descendant.

'I'd just assumed that is how it would be arranged—but, as I said earlier, if you want to run things differently, that's entirely up to you.'

There was an awkward silence, then Cressida said, 'You asked me what I know about the Priory?'

Sir Piers nodded.

'I did some homework before I came—though of course I don't know all that much, just the bare outlines, really. I discovered that the house was built on land owned by a powerful monastery dissolved by Henry VIII, or rather *for* Henry by Sir Roger there.' They both glanced up at his likeness. Put Sir Piers into Tudor costume, Cressida thought, and he might step back into the frame . . .

'Is that the sum total of your knowledge, Miss Heaton?' The tone was amused rather than reproving.

'Well . . .' She hesitated. 'I did try to see what else I could find out about your family, but there wasn't a lot of information in our local library, and you didn't give me a lot of time.'

Sir Piers uttered a short laugh. 'It's hardly surprising. Our family has not been noted for great distinction in any field. We've tended to keep ourselves to ourselves, which has not helped much in contributing to the state of the coffers.'

'I don't see . . .' Cressida began, puzzled.

'No great public office, therefore no golden handshakes from grateful monarchs—and no peerage either, or valuable gifts that could be sold later. We didn't make much of a contribution to the industrial revolution, so no profit there.' He gazed round the faces of his ancestors. 'Sir Edward there . . .' he pointed to a severely attired gentleman with long, fair hair '. . .he tried to sit on the fence as long as he could during the Civil War, but East Anglia was mostly under Cromwell's influence—he came from these parts, so it was hardly surprising—and that saved the house from damage, but as you'll see when we go round, the house has hardly been altered at all over the centuries . . . so the lack of riches hasn't been entirely a disadvantage.'

Without warning he turned and moved swiftly across the Hall and opened the door in the panelling through which he had made his earlier, scary appearance.

Cressida hurried to keep up with him and ducked under the lintel to find herself at the foot of a wide, wooden staircase.

'Servants' door,' Sir Piers explained briefly. 'You'll find them all over the place—they were expected to be as invisible as possible, and they used passages between the panelling to get around the house. The kitchens are through there . . .' he pointed to another door in the corner '. . . but we'll go upstairs first.'

He bounded up the shallow treads with a lithe grace that left Cressida way behind. She got the distinct impression that he was trying to get this whole rather distasteful tour over as quickly as possible. She finally caught up with him at the end of what he told her was called the South Gallery.

'Where the ladies used to exercise on wet days, wasn't it?' Cressida asked, her spirits lifting at the sight of this room so much lighter than the Great Hall downstairs. Large, leaded windows ran the whole length of one side which a quick look informed her overlooked the courtyard.

'And they could look out and see if anyone was coming to call,' she added, her imagination running riot with colourful images of crinolined ladies and powdered gentlemen filling the place with laughter and music. 'What parties they must have had up here . . .' She allowed herself a frivolous pirouette. 'Do you often . . .?'

'No,' Sir Piers countered dourly. 'I don't know what picture you have of life here, but I've already told you there's no one here except myself.' A twisted smile barely reached his eyes. 'You can't have much of a party with one—though you may have gathered I'm not much of a one for socialising.'

Cressida turned from her scrutiny of the view through the windows to face him, her own eyes illuminated with a sudden flash of inspiration.

'It would be quite a way to launch the Priory, though, wouldn't it? A reception of some kind—or, better still,' she added, warming to the idea, 'a ball. A fancy dress ball, perhaps.' She clasped her hands together to stop them reaching out to grasp his arm in her enthusiasm. 'What do you think—isn't it a great idea?'

'I've told you before—I have no interest in your ideas.' Sir Piers tightened his jaw and turned away.

'But you wouldn't be against it?' Cressida persisted, hurrying after him as he strode off along the polished floor. 'And you would put in an appearance, at least? I can just imagine it, you in fancy dress. You look so like those portraits, downstairs—it'd be fantastic! Sir Roger come to life!'

'I'll thank you to leave me out of it, and any other cheapjack scheme you might hatch up.'

Sir Piers swung round and glared at Cressida with such ferocity that she flinched back, almost physically afraid of the antipathy she read on his face.

'I'm sorry,' she stammered, her cheeks flushing with embarrassment. She certainly had overstepped the mark this time. 'I only thought it might be a good idea . . . the publicity and everything.' She smiled ruefully, forcing herself to meet his hostile gaze. 'I'm afraid I let my imagination run away with me sometimes.'

He stared at her for a moment in a grimly disapproving silence. 'The Priory can do without that kind of publicity. There's been quite enough . . .' A look almost of desperation crossed his face, then, without another word, he walked off along the passage that ran at right angles to the Gallery.

'Bedrooms,' he explained curtly, opening the first door they came to. 'And closets.' He halted at the head of another staircase and nodded towards the rooms at the farthest end of the wing. 'My room's along there.'

Cressida stood at the top of the stairs looking back along the way they had come. It would be easy to guide visitors . . . into the Great Hall, up the main staircase, along the Gallery and down here without disturbing Sir Piers at all, if that was what he wanted. But he still hadn't explained why he needed the money the visitors would bring.

'You said you would tell me . . .' She stopped, not wishing to offend him yet again, but he seemed not to want to take advantage of the opening she had offered him. His fingers beat a gentle tattoo on the banisters as he waited to see how she was going to phrase the end of the sentence although, she thought crossly, he must know what it was she wanted to say. She stared at his hand, frowning. Maybe it was some kind of test. Well, try straight talking.

'You said you would tell me how your family got into financial difficulties,' she reminded him bluntly, raising her eyes to catch a gleam of what might, possibly, be approval in those inscrutable grey depths—gold-flecked, she noticed for the first time—as he held her gaze.

'I did, didn't I?'

Again a silence, but one which Cressida dared not break. This was clearly a painful subject and one which would need all her tact.

'Let's go into the garden,' Sir Piers said surprisingly, leading the way down, adding softly in an undertone Cressida wasn't sure whether she was meant to hear, 'I can talk more easily out of doors—this place has too many memories.'

'Oh, isn't that beautiful?' Cressida's eyes sparkled with delight as she followed Sir Piers round the end of the west wing and she saw the gardens for the first time.

Smooth, green lawns swept away to meet a wooded area consisting mainly of beech trees now at their most enchanting, tinged with the fresh, pale green of spring. In the foreground was an area of small flower-beds formally divided up into geometric patterns separated by low, clipped hedges. Someone had been working there recently, preparing the ground for later planting.

'Surely you don't look after all *this* by yourself?' Cressida waved her arm expansively to embrace the whole landscape. 'No one could cope with that amount of land without some sort of help.'

Sir Piers bent to pull out a weed which had dared poke its head up through the hedge, and when he straightened up Cressida saw the first hint of a quite different side to his character. At last he was smiling, a real, unselfconscious smile which illuminated not only his face but seemed to pervade his whole body so that the hunched-up shoulders relaxed, and he thrust his hands deep into his pockets with an almost boyish gesture. Years seemed to slip from him in that one instant—if only he could always be like this, Cressida thought. This was where his heart was, as she had suspected earlier from his caged-up demeanour in the study.

'I do most of it,' he replied almost proudly, and with a real grin. 'A couple of chaps do come in from the village to help with the mowing, but I like to take charge of the real gardening.'

He gazed lovingly at the formal garden in front of them. 'Over the winter I've been trying to restore this according to the original design. There are some old prints in the study—I'll show them to you if you're interested . . . but it had been allowed to go to rack and ruin.'

The gloomy cloud of an unwelcome memory blotted out the sunny expression as the dark brows knitted together again. Cressida couldn't repress a sigh—she might have known it had been too good to last.

'By the way,' she said in an attempt to bring the conversation back to less dark topics, 'I couldn't help noticing that there weren't any portraits of women back in the Priory. There must have been some, surely—they can't all have been so plain that no one wanted them painted?'

Severe lines meshed round his mouth as her feeble joke misfired.

'Far from it,' came the harsh reply. 'Some of the best pictures were of the Aylward wives and daughters—a van Dyck, a couple of Knellers and a small Gainsborough, but they have been sold.'

'Oh, how dreadful!' Cressida exclaimed in dismay. 'Whoever needed the money so badly that they would do that?'

There was a bleak pause. 'I did.'

Cressida was appalled. 'I am so sorry—I didn't know, or I would never have mentioned it.'

Sir Piers laughed bitterly. 'How could you know? But I'll tell you—you need to know the full story, anyway

. . . and then it will be done.'

Cressida cast longing eyes towards a stone bench set in the shelter of the wall—it had been a long and tiring day—but Sir Piers seemed oblivious to her needs as he stared out with unseeing eyes towards the distant woods.

'It's a long story,' he said quietly, 'but you don't need to know all the details of what went wrong . . .' He broke off into a painful silence.

'If you'd rather not . . .' Cressida began, but Sir Piers shook his head impatiently.

'No, it's best you should hear it from me. You'll only get a garbled version from people in the village, and really I suppose there's nothing remarkable or scandalous about what happened. It's only too commonplace in families like mine—but you never think it will happen to you.'

'Death-duties?' Cressida did her best to sound well informed.

Sir Piers grunted assent. 'Inheritance tax, it's called now—and, coupled with an improvidence and extravagance which would sound amusingly romantic if you were reading about the eighteenth century, but when it's nearer to home . . . when it's your own brother . . .' He spat out the last words with a violence which made Cressida start back, but after a moment he recovered himself and continued in a calmer tone, though still shot through with bitterness, 'You may not know, Miss Heaton, that I am only the second son. I never imagined I would have the responsibility of caring for the Priory. I love it, you see—I've always loved it more than anything in the world, and from my earliest childhood I knew it would never be mine.' His hands clenched into tight fists and Cressida could sense the fierce passion coursing through his veins as the space between them became charged with an electric current of suppressed emotion.

'My elder brother, Hugo, never had any feeling for the place, and when our father died and he took over the Priory, he made it quite clear that he would only do the absolute minimum in the way of upkeep. He regarded it as nothing more than a millstone round his neck, his one aim in life being to have a good time and spend as much money as he could lay his greedy hands on.'

Fierce resentment sounded in every word and Cressida's heart went out to him in sympathy. She wished devoutly that she had never raised the subject, although, as he had pointed out, she did need to know the full story, if only to prevent her asking more painful questions in the future. She stood motionless by his side, knowing any interruption would only prolong his distress.

'I couldn't bear to live here, seeing it all decay in front of my eyes, so I packed up and turned myself into what you might call a professional traveller. That way I could go where I liked, writing to earn my keep . . . my wants weren't—aren't—very demanding, and I managed well enough.'

So that accounts for the tan, Cressida thought, but Sir Piers hadn't finished.

'Then Hugo went too far; he married a wife even more extravagant than he was—the lovely Miriam . . .' bitterness grated in his voice ' . . . and together they ran up debts you wouldn't believe. He began to gamble to try to recoup his losses—but of course he couldn't . . . and finally, when there was no way out, he died.'

'He didn't . . .?' Cressida could scarcely bring herself to ask the question, but Sir Piers headed her off.

'No, he didn't take his own life. Even his death was conspicuous by its lack of dignity. He fell off a yacht in a drunken stupor during a particularly wild party given by one of his so-called jet-setting friends, and drowned. It was as simple and as sordid as that.'

Cressida could think of nothing to say, but he still had more to add.

'There were no children, which was about the only gift Hugo managed to confer on humanity, whether by accident or design I neither know nor care—except that by dying childless he made me heir to all this . . .' He swept a semi circle in front of him ' . . . and with an enormous sum of money to pay off.'

'The pictures?' Cressida breathed, daring at last to lift her eyes to his. Calmer now he had told her, he nodded.

'I sold those to pay off their debts—and his precious wife—and now I'm only left with the government's slice of the cake, and that's no mere sliver, I can tell you.' He managed a bitter laugh.

'So that's where I come in?' Cressida put in gently.

'I don't know whether opening the Priory to visitors will raise even a fraction of what's needed—but I must try to save it somehow. The thought of selling it, letting someone turn it into a hotel or a conference centre . . .' His voice ended on a desperate note and he thrust his hands deep into his pockets, the old, hunched look coming back.

'I'll do everything I can to help,' Cressida promised him, suddenly and rather alarmingly aware of the responsibility that lay in her hands. If she had known all it was going to involve, she might have had second thoughts about applying for this job, but—she allowed herself a little sigh of resignation—she wasn't one to turn away from a challenge, especially before she had even begun. If it all got too much, well, she wasn't committed for life. She could always abdicate in favour of someone with more experience.

She looked round at the peaceful green landscape and the ancient trees planted so long ago by men of vision for the delight of future generations they would never know, and gradually a sense of pride began to take root within her. The future of the Priory had been laid at her unsuspecting feet, and not only the Priory . . . a man's future was at stake, too.

She shifted her gaze, unobserved, to the tall figure whose broad back was turned to her. Not for the first time and, she knew, it wouldn't be the last either, Cressida considered the strange contradictions that made up this man with whom she was to work—and live—in such close proximity. She recalled the word her father had used to describe the Priory. Forlorn. Well, it wasn't just the house which looked forlorn, but its owner too as he stood, oblivious to her presence and lost in his own sad thoughts. Cressida longed to put her arms round him, to hold him close in comfort . . . her heart began to beat faster as she imagined that hard, muscular body against her own, her fingers touching the smooth skin of his cheek . . .

She brought herself up sharply. That way madness lies, she chided herself— and the sack. There must be no nonsense of that kind—she was here to do a job, a difficult, responsible job, and that was all.

And as far as the job was concerned there were still lots of matters she had to get settled before she could make a start. Best broach the subject now, while she had the chance. She took a deep breath.

'There are still one or two things . . .' But her good, businesslike intentions were abruptly betrayed by a purely physical reaction to the stress of the day. A gust of chill wind whipped round the corner of the building, making Cressida shiver with cold just as Sir Piers turned back towards her. He glanced at his watch and raised his eyebrows in surprise. 'You're cold,' he stated, 'and I must apologise for keeping you out here so long. I dare say you're hungry as well. Come on—we'll go back indoors.'

They walked back towards the main entrance side by side.

'I'll show you where the kitchen is, and leave you to help yourself to some tea, if I may. I have one or two things to see to. Mrs Bryant always sees there is some cake in the tin . . . a weakness of mine, I'm afraid.' He permitted himself a faint smile before continuing, hesitating awkwardly as he sought for a way to avoid sounding actually rude. 'About meals . . .'

Cressida came to his rescue, already knowing him well enough to be sure he would prefer to eat alone.

'Just show me where the kitchen is, and I can easily fend for myself.'

Sir Piers shot her a quick look, grateful for her instinctive understanding.

'Mrs Bryant always gets my lunch, when I'm here—and I make my own supper . . . sandwiches, eggs—that sort of thing. I'm quite used to looking after myself.'

Cressida nodded. 'I can do the same, then we won't be tied to a timetable. Much the most sensible arrangement.'

They had reached the kitchen by now, a huge room, stone-flagged like the rest of the ground floor except for the living-rooms, with a modern electric cooker and fridge somewhat incongruously situated between a shallow, old-fashioned sink and an enormous dresser.

A scrubbed pine table took up the centre of the room, the sort that in Cressida's part of the country would cost hundreds of pounds in a fashionable antique shop. Here it didn't look trendy, just right, like the solid chairs round it. For all its vastness, the kitchen had a homely look to it with its polished brass and pot plants—Mrs Bryant's touch, surely. Cressida felt cheered. At least there would be one person to share the occasional chat with. There was a tray laid with tea things and an electric kettle stood on the draining-board. Cressida filled it and plugged it in to boil.

Sir Piers was still hovering in the doorway, obviously wanting to make his escape back to his room.

'Shall I bring you a cup?' Cressida enquired, hand poised over the tea caddy. 'And some cake?'

His face lit up. 'That would be kind.' He paused. 'Oh—and there's no need to worry about supper this evening. We . . . Mrs Bryant . . . thought you would be hungry after the journey and settling in, and has prepared dinner for both of us. I should be very pleased if you would join me. About seven?'

Without waiting for a reply he turned on his heel and disappeared along the passage. Cressida grinned to herself. Poor Sir Piers! Two pounds to a penny Mrs Bryant had suggested they eat together—bullied him, more like. She wondered how long Mrs Bryant had been working for him. Maybe she would be able to give her some hints on how best to cope with his strange, mercurial moods . . . she sincerely hoped so.

The kettle's lid began to rattle. It was an old model, not designed to turn itself off, and Cressida unplugged it and made the tea. Once she had taken Sir Piers his cup she could at last put her feet up in her room and collect her thoughts together before preparing herself for the slightly alarming prospect of an intimate dinner with her employer.

CHAPTER THREE

CRESSIDA poured herself a cup of tea, sank her teeth into a large slice of Mrs Bryant's fruitcake and settled herself comfortably in the less battered of the two armchairs in her 'office'. It was surprising just how comfortable it was, considering its age and the fact it creaked alarmingly every time she moved.

In fact, the chair was a kind of symbol of all that was peculiar about her new circumstances . . . It seemed extraordinary to be sitting here in a valuable antique in a stately home, though in anything but stately surroundings—she gazed round the sparsely furnished room which, even with her own possessions added to the minimum of furniture provided by Sir Piers, presented a pretty bleak picture.

Where had they found those curtains? Hand-me-down, or rather cut-me-down faded crimson brocade filched from one of the disused bedrooms, no doubt. On the stone floor were one or two threadbare rugs—old, certainly, possibly antique as well, as far as she knew. No doubt the best they could find after the ravages perpetrated by the profligate Hugo and his wife.

Cressida sighed. It was certainly not the lap of luxury, and something would have to be done to smarten the place up a bit, especially if she were to invite people to come and see her here on business. She could hardly be expected to transact everything by telephone.

Telephone? That was a point—was there one? She looked round curiously without bothering to get up, for she knew the answer already. Of course there wasn't, nor a typewriter, and she would need both . . . something to ask Sir Piers over dinner.

What an extraordinary man he was! You'd think he would want to know exactly what she was planning . . . this was his home, after all, and feeling the way he did about it, too. Although she had met him only hours ago, she already felt she knew enough about him to fill a book.

She lay back in the chair, considering his appearance. Tall, deceptively muscular under his shabby clothes . . . she recalled the way he'd swung her luggage up into his arms, the lightness of his step as he ran up the stairs. The deep tan which had so surprised her was now easily explained by his way of life—a traveller and a writer. That was something else she could draw on as a topic of conversation later, and she would need all the ideas she could muster if they weren't to sit in an awkward silence all evening. She had never met a man so disinclined for company.

Had he always been like that, she wondered, or did it have something to do with his unhappy relationship with his brother and sister-in-law? What was her name—Miriam, wasn't it?

Cressida frowned. Apart from this Miriam, he had never mentioned any women, not even his mother. Her ever fertile imagination began to concoct a deliciously romantic web around the figure of the unhappy second son, burning with a passionate love for the ancestral home he would never inherit, maybe ignored by both parents in favour of his spoilt elder brother, sent away to school and finally taking refuge in a solitary, rootless existence, making a meagre livelihood from his writing.

Nor had he ever mentioned a wife, though surely with those distinctive, yet aloof, good looks he must have attracted considerable attention during his travels. That enigmatic reserve would present a challenge to any woman with whom he came in contact, even break a few hearts too, she wouldn't be surprised.

And what of her own heart? Those striking features certainly had the power to make it beat faster. Cressida's inward eye dwelt on the smooth, fair hair, such a contrast to the sunburnt complexion and dark brows, the grey, sea-cold eyes, glinting gold when he allowed his suppressed emotions to break through the mask of inscrutability. Undemonstrative he might be, but those few flashes of fury when he was talking about his brother told her more about his inner feelings than volumes of words would have done.

She would have to be careful—it would never do to fall in love with him. Her own emotions must stay on a strictly even keel, matching his own cool detachment.

Well, Cressida Heaton, she told herself, you wanted a challenge and there's no doubt you have found one. And the job hasn't even got under way yet. Take things one at a time—and the first thing is to decide what to wear for dinner.

She frowned as she studied the contents of her wardrobe. What was it Sir Piers had said? 'I would be pleased if you would join me for dinner.'

Did that mean a formal affair, one either end of a huge polished table eating frugally from priceless porcelain, or would it be a cosier affair, helping themselves from saucepans in the kitchen, Sir Piers still in his sloppy sweater and cords? Neither scenario seemed quite right; it would be somewhere between both extremes. Whatever his natural and reclusive tendencies, Sir Piers, she felt sure, would do the right thing when it came to entertaining guests, however humble.

That brought her back to where she had started.

What to wear? Nothing too formal, but something that would show she appreciated his hospitable gesture, and, she decided practically, something warm! She doubted whether any part of the Priory had been modernised to the extent of having central heating— certainly she had seen no evidence of it so far.

Cressida pulled on a soft, cream sweater and pleated wool skirt. How she wished she had a long mirror—she would have to make do with the small looking-glass on the chest of drawers, which was all there was.

She stooped to get a closer look at her reflection, tilting the mirror so that she could get some idea of what Sir Piers would see when she went along to join him. Her dark hair fell forward, and impatiently she scooped it behind her head in a makeshift knot. She rather liked the effect, enhancing as it did the oval shape of her face and showing off her long neck to considerable advantage. She couldn't spare the time to fix it like this just now, but for a more formal occasion . . . She let the thick tresses fall free again and pulled at her sweater lest it cling too revealingly to the shapely curves of the body beneath. She had no desire to give Sir Piers the wrong impression—feminine, yes, but businesslike and efficient as well, or the fragile equilibrium of their relationship might so easily be upset.

The study door was ajar, and Cressida knocked gently. There was no reply, so, after a moment's pause, she pushed it open cautiously and went in.

Sir Piers was nowhere to be seen, and the unnerving silence gave her no clue as to where he might be, so she crossed the room to the fireplace where a welcome log fire now crackled cheerfully. She stood warming her back and took a longer look at the room where Sir Piers obviously spent most of his time when he wasn't out of doors, hoping she might learn something more of his interests. Where he did his travelling, for instance.

The large desk was still as orderly as it had been on her earlier visit, the few papers arranged in neat piles. Nothing there to give even a hint of what made him tick. What about the books, though—and wasn't that a word processor on the table behind the door?

Intrigued, Cressida began a tour of inspection, squatting down to read the titles on the lower shelves, and there, almost hidden from view, was a short row of volumes by just the one author: Piers Aylward.

She pulled one out.

'Are you interested in travel, Miss Heaton?'

Cressida almost unbalanced as she spun round, startled by his silent approach. She rose unsteadily to her feet, clutching the book in her hand.

'You quite frightened me,' she reproached him lightly. 'I see I shall have to get used to being startled by your sudden entrances.'

She moved back into the middle of the room, smiling, her heart giving an unexpected jump as she saw his eyes widen fractionally, the glint of gold betraying his male instincts as he registered the curves of her body almost, she was sure, against his will. Then the mask fell again as swiftly as it had been raised, and she dropped her own gaze to the book she was holding.

'I'm sorry,' she said. 'I hope you don't think I was prying, but I couldn't help noticing this . . . and the others.' She gestured towards the shelves. 'I suppose I couldn't borrow it?'

Sir Piers nodded, allowing himself a brief smile of pleasure. 'Of course—and any other book you might like to read.' He hesitated, then added awkwardly, 'I hope you will feel this is your home, Miss Heaton—while you are working here. I . . . I want you to be as comfortable as you can.'

Cressida's spirits lifted with a surge of optimism. 'In that case, could you call me Cressida, do you think—unless you think that's too informal? I don't want to seem presumptuous, but if there are only the two of us here mostly, it would sound less forbidding somehow. . .' Her voice trailed off. Had she gone too far?

'Cressida.' The deep voice lingered over the name. 'It's not a very common name, is it? There's Shakespeare's heroine, of course . . .' He paused reflectively. 'Yes, I'll call you Cressida, though I warn you, I might forget,' he added with a burst of engaging candour. 'Formality is more in my nature, but I'll try.'

Would he unbend even further, Cressida wondered, watching him and ask her to drop the title from his own name, in private at least? But the idea didn't even appear to occur to him. He walked over to a cupboard in the far corner.

'Sherry, Miss . . . Cressida?'

'Yes, thank you.'

Under cover of examining the book still in her hand, she directed a surreptitious glance at him from beneath her lashes as he brought out a decanter and two glasses which he placed carefully on his desk. He had indeed changed in honour of the occasion out of his old threadbare cords into an unremarkable pair of grey flannel trousers, but the jacket, although not in the first flush of youth, must have been made by a first-class tailor. Stretched smoothly over his broad shoulders, it accentuated the straight lines of his back, making his lean body seem even taller and more strongly muscled than it had appeared under the disguise of the baggy sweater.

She might have known he would no more have contemplated appearing for dinner in his ol clothes than . . . than opening up the Priory for a pop festival.

The absurdity of both ideas made her grin, although, now she'd thought of it, it wasn't such a bad notion at that. It would certainly put the Priory on the map, and would be following precedents set at some of the statelier homes, too. They could certainly make a lot of money that way, but apart from the fact that it was clearly out of the question—Sir Piers would ever wear the idea, not in a million years—and even though he wanted nothing to do with opening up his house, she could hardly go ahead without his permission on something as big as that.

Also, she knew nothing whatever about pop festivals.

'Something amusing you, Miss . . . Cressida?' Sir Piers held out a glass to her, and as she took it, their fingers brushed momentarily. She shot him a swift glance. I'm winning, she thought—not so much as a tremor of alarm on that serious face. It was like trying to gain the trust of a wild animal . . . one step at at time, nothing too hasty.

'Well . . .?' he prompted, leaning his back against the mantelpiece as he looked down on Cressida where she perched on the arm of one of the old leather armchairs, sipping decorously at the sherry.

'I beg your pardon?' she began, then remembered. 'Oh, yes . . . I just had a passing thought . . . a vision of the Priory being used for a pop festival,' she continued with greater daring, 'but . . .'

She was not allowed to continue.

'If you think . . .' Sir Piers exploded. Cressida went pink—she had gone too far again. He didn't know her well enough yet to know when she was joking. It had been stupid of her.

'No, I'm sorry—I wasn't being serious, honestly, Sir Piers. I was just letting my imagination run away with me again. I'm afraid it does, sometimes.'

Sir Piers turned away and stared into the flickering firelight. Cressida cursed herself for her ill-timed frivolity. The Priory was sacred ground, and she must learn not to make jokes where it was concerned. She took a large sip of her drink.

'I do apologise,' she repeated. 'Please believe me, nothing could be further from my thoughts.' Again, all her instincts prompted her to leap up and put her hand on that arm lying stiffly along the mantelpiece, but she knew that any gesture of the sort was strictly out of bounds.

She stared helplessly at the bent head—it was so difficult to say the right thing to him . . . and she had thought he was beginning to relax in her company. Conversation must be kept on a business footing quite definitely in future—no personal remarks, and no jokes.

At last Sir Piers straightened up, glancing briefly in her direction.

'I'll go and see that everything is ready,' he said without emotion. 'Please help yourself to more sherry if you would like some.'

He strode swiftly out of the room as though glad to escape, and his footfalls soon died away, leaving Cressida alone once more.

Conversation was sticky to begin with at dinner, but gradually, under the influence of Mrs Bryant's delicious food and a rather grand bottle of wine produced by Sir Piers— 'One of the few remaining,' he told her wistfully, 'from a once splendid cellar ravaged by my brother for his extravagant parties,' —Cressida was glad to see the taut lines relax once more on her employer's face, and she began to draw him out on the subject of his travels.

The surroundings helped too, she decided, staring

round at the small, elegant dining-room decorated by contrast with the rest of the house in eighteenth-century fashion.

The pale Chinese carpet complemented the lighter wainscoting and hand-painted wallpaper, giving an overall effect of elegant charm. Gone was the heavy oak furniture; the mahogany chairs and table glowed with centuries of care and polish, reflecting the sparkle from the candelabra and silverware gracing the table. Someone—she didn't like to enquire whether it was Mrs Bryant's idea or whether Sir Piers had had a hand in it too—had gone to a lot of trouble on her behalf, for she was quite sure he did not eat in this style when he was alone. She allowed herself to feel just a little flattered . . . this once, at least.

By putting in what she hoped were reasonably intelligent remarks and questions, Cressida did her part in keeping the talk flowing. No wonder the poor man felt cooped up here, she thought, listening to him describing an expedition he had made in the high Andes, keeping well away from the tourist areas and from as much human contact as possible. And yet, he was so devoted to his home, you would think he would want a hand in the plan to open it up to visitors, however reclusive his nature.

She watched his brown hands gesticulating as he described the mountain landscape he loved, his eyes alive and almost humorous in animated response to one of her questions. For a moment he had clearly forgotten his current problems, maybe was almost unaware of her presence except as an interested audience—then the pretty clock on the sideboard chimed the hour, and, Cinderella-like, the enchantment vanished, leaving behind only a memory of freedom as he came face to face with reality once more.

'I do hope I'm not boring you?' He smiled ruefully and gave a sigh of regret. 'I do tend to get carried away, but I must get back to earth, I suppose, and Clarewood in particular. There must be things you want to ask, about your job, for instance?'

Cressida gave an answering smile of sympathy.

'We can leave it till after dinner. It seems a shame to spoil the occasion by talking shop. Tell me about this room instead. Has it always been a dining-room, and whose idea was it originally to decorate it in this style?'

Sir Piers nodded towards the pair of portraits on the wall opposite. 'Sir John and Lady Maria—two of my very favourite ancestors. She was a lady of great taste and distinction, and whatever other pictures have to be sold, I am determined these shall stay here.'

It was difficult to see them clearly in the candlelight, but Cressida promised herself a closer look in the daylight. There was something else on her mind, though, and this seemed as good a moment to bring it up as any other.

'I know I said we shouldn't talk shop, but while I remember . . . I shall need to know as much as possible about your family,' she went on hesitantly. 'People will be interested, you know—really interested—and it's the little human details which make ordinary visitors care for a place. They will be our bread and butter, and although I do realise how distasteful it will be to have them all over your home, we do want them to enjoy their visit, and tell their friends, too. I know that's why I like going to stately homes—it puts flesh on to the bare bones of history.'

She wasn't sure whether she had made the phrase up or had read it somewhere, but it made Sir Piers look sharply at her, almost as though he were noticing her as an individual in her own right for the first time. His eyes glinted as they met hers across the flickering candles.

'As it happens, I have written a short history of the Priory, and the Aylwards, for you to use—you can read it through, and we can discuss later any extra details you think it may be necessary to add. There are a few documents—old histories, diaries and so on—which you might be interested to see. Then you can add your own personal comments to my—bare bones!' he finished drily.

So he's not quite so uninterested as he likes to make out, Cressida decided with satisfaction. Maybe, now that he had credited her with at least some intelligence, he might eventually be persuaded not to hold himself quite so aloof from any schemes she came up with.

They had finished the meal now, and Sir Piers was beginning to show signs of withdrawing into himself again, sitting silently twirling the stem of his empty glass between his long, brown fingers.

Cressida cleared her throat.

'Shall I take these things out to the kitchen? I could make the coffee, too, if you'll show me where everything is, then bring it along to the study.' She smiled across at him. 'It was very good of you—and Mrs Bryant—to go to all this trouble, and it's the least I can do in return.'

Sir Piers stood up and came round to her side of the table, courteously pulling her chair away as she got to her feet. She turned to face him, her pulses quickening instinctively at his closeness. He was tall, but so was she, and as he bent over the chair their eyes met directly and just for one heart-stopping moment she sensed just a glimmer of response in the gold-flecked depths. If only . . . but any contact was as yet so fragile, like a spider's web that could be destroyed by the least clumsy, ill-timed movement.

Cressida quickly lowered her gaze to hide any hint of her own emotions, and began the prosaic task of collecting the plates together.

She quite enjoyed pottering round the vast kitchen on her own, loading the dishwasher—one twentieth-century addition she was glad to see in strange contrast to the old-fashioned sink—and making coffee in a new filter machine. It was nice to have something practical and positive to do at last, though she reflected ruefully as she went in search of the coffee-cups that in a few weeks' time she would no doubt look back on that particular thought in disbelief. With no help forthcoming from her employer, all the work would fall solely on her shoulders. There was clearly little or no money available for assistance, though she would have to find some local people to help as guides, ticket sellers and so on. Mrs Bryant might well be a valuable source of information in that area. She was quite looking forward to meeting her. At least, if they got on, she would be someone to talk to.

Cressida picked up the tray and looked round. It would never do to leave the kitchen untidy. No, everything was shipshape. She turned the lights off and went back to the study. The door was open and she paused on the threshold to push it open with her foot—and stopped.

Sir Piers was sitting slumped in a chair, his long hand shading his eyes in a attitude of utter weariness and despair. For the first time Cressida saw the project through his eyes, and something of what he must be feeling communicated itself to her through the dejected pose of his body. Her heart went out to him. How would she, or anybody else, for that matter, like the prospect of putting up with a complete stranger, however sympathetic, living under the same roof—a stranger whose sole aim was to bring in as many people as possible to tramp round your home, making comments, laughing, criticising and paying out money to recoup the losses incurred by the excesses of a dissolute brother?

Quietly she entered the room and placed the tray on a small table near him. Was she expected to stay? She filled the two cups and waited, not wishing to disturb him. At last he looked up.

'Coffee, Sir Piers?'

He nodded and took the cup she offered him, refusing milk and sugar. Cressida remained standing, looking down at the bent head and wondering what to do next. Did he feel he had fulfilled all the duties expected of him as host by entertaining her to dinner? She made up her mind.

'I'll go back to my room now, Sir Piers. It's been a long day and I'll be glad of an early night.'

Was that relief she read on his face?

'Thank you for a very pleasant evening,' Cressida went on, turning to go. 'Will I see you tomorrow? There are one or two practical details I need to sort out before I can begin my real planning.'

Sir Piers could not disguise a faint sigh of resignation. 'Yes, I'll be here.' He rose to his feet and held out his hand. 'It has been a pleasure to meet you, Miss . . . Cressida. I hope you sleep well.'

Cressida put her hand in his, responding to his polite words and the firm grasp of his fingers with a warm smile. 'I'll do my best for you, Sir Piers; I do understand what this must mean for you, and I promise I won't bother you more than I have to. It may all turn out better than you think,' she added hopefully.

Sir Piers' lips compressed into a bleak smile. 'Thank you,' he said as he released her hand. 'I'm glad one of us is optimistic about the outcome of this affair. We'll have to see, won't we?'

It was only as she was getting into bed that Cressida realised that her strange, unhappy, withdrawn employer had never asked her one question about herself, her interests or her relationships . . . not a single thing.

She gave a deep sigh. The sooner she came to terms with the fact that he meant it when he said he was not interested in other people, the better for her own peace of mind, and the job she had come here to do. And, on that melancholy reflection, she fell into an exhausted sleep.

CHAPTER FOUR

THE BED in her spartan room proved to be surprisingly comfortable, and Cressida slept like a log, gradually surfacing to the by now familiar and almost tangible silence.

It was still only seven o'clock, and she stretched luxuriously under the bedclothes, taking the opportunity to go over in her mind all the strange events of the previous day. The scene was now set for the play to begin, with her as both actor and director . . . more a one-woman show, actually, she decided, continuing the metaphor, since the star had pulled out of the production.

She could understand why Sir Piers wanted nothing to do with the visitors whom it was her job to encourage to come to the Priory, but then she hardly imagined that any owners of stately homes exactly relished throwing them open to the public, let alone having the safari parks, fun-fairs and other publicity stunts that brought in the money to save their homes for posterity. She *would* have to choose the one owner who flatly refused to co-operate with his adminstrator, although maybe to be in sole command might in the end prove to have some advantages.

The whole thing presented a pretty daunting picture, and it was with great reluctance that Cressida finally climbed out of bed on this, her first day in her new job. She went over to the window to pull back the curtains—cautiously, just in case there was anyone out in the gardens who might catch sight of her standing there in her nightdress. Her room looked out over the grounds on the opposite side of the house to the formal garden where her employer spent most of his time. Here there was only rolling, empty parkland stretching as far as the eye could see, with clumps of venerable beeches and oaks, and in the distance what looked like a ruined building of some kind.

Could that be the remains of the original Priory? She must find out—romantic ruins might be valuable as an added attraction.

Cressida drew in her breath sharply, suddenly aware of the cold. It had been warm enough in bed, but the room was chill with the unheated air of centuries, and she hurried to put some clothes on. Nothing had been mentioned about breakfast, the day before, but she assumed it was a help-yourself-in-the-kitchen meal, like all the others. She wondered whether Mrs Bryant had arrived yet.

I hope we get on, she thought, or it's going to be exceedingly lonely here. She had been so used to working and living with other people that the solitude might get to her if she didn't find some compatible soul to talk to.

Cressida made her way to the kitchen, trying not to stop and listen at every step, and doing her best to think of this imposing building as her home.

I live here, she said to herself, passing the study and the passage which led to the Great Hal with the rows of disapproving Aylward ancestors. 'I live here,' she repeated out loud, and if I make a noise, at least it shows there's something going on here at last. It was as though the whole Priory had fallen asleep and had been waiting for her to wake it up again.

There was no one to be seen in the kitchen, but Sir

Piers had obviously already had his breakfast, judging from the half-filled jug of coffee keeping warm on the filter machine's hot-plate. Marmalade and butter were on the table, and Cressida foraged around, finding some bread in an old stone crock. She made herself two slices of toast and while she was searching for a plate and a cup she heard footsteps approaching—fast, busy footsteps quite unlike Sir Piers' silent tread.

She looked up expectantly as a small, wiry woman of about forty-five pushed open the door and came bustling towards her.

'Miss Heaton?' she enquired with a friendly smile. 'I'm Mary Bryant.'

Cressida's spirits lifted immediately at the sight of the open, sensible features, and firm grasp of Mary Bryant's hand.

'I can't tell you how relieved I am to meet you,' Cressida confided frankly, dividing what was left of the coffee between the two of them.

Mary Bryant pulled up a chair and shot her a perceptive glance.

'Come as a bit of a surprise, I dare say—all this, and Sir Piers thrown in?'

Cressida nodded. 'It's so quiet . . . I don't know what I was expecting—and Sir Piers isn't exactly what you'd call outgoing, is he?'

Mary laughed and drank some coffee, considering Cressida over the edge of her cup.

'Forgive me for saying so, but you're not very old, are you? Have you had a lot of experience in this kind of work?'

Cressida shook her head ruefully. 'None,' she acknowledged, 'and I'm beginning to wonder what I've let myself in for . . . though being unprepared isn't altogether my fault. Sir Piers never even asked me for an interview, you know. I did tell him in my letter how old I was, and what I'd done up till now. He could have appointed someone else.'

She got up and took her breakfast things over to the sink. 'Still, my guess is that he wanted to avoid meeting the applicants. He did actually say he knew he wasn't any good with people . . .' She paused, not wanting to sound as though she was criticising him to someone who had known him a lot longer than she had.

Mary came over to join her, picking up a teatowel to dry the plates.

'Have you known Sir Piers long?' Cressida asked. 'And in case you think I'm prying, I do know the background to all this, and why I'm here. Sir Piers told me yesterday about his brother and everything.' She frowned at the memory. 'Has he always been so withdrawn and difficult to talk to? So . . .' she sought the right word '. . . so on his guard?'

'I've lived in the village all my life,' Mary told her, 'and Piers was always reckoned to be the quiet one, even as a boy. His father, Sir Robert, was a nice enough man—a typical kind of country squire, I suppose you'd call him—and his mother . . . she was a lovely woman . . .'

She broke off to get a duster and vacuum cleaner from a cupboard on the far side of the room before tying on a pinafore.

'Sir Piers never mentioned his mother,' Cressida commented.

'No . . . well . . .' Mary hesitated. 'She died when he was only a lad. Cancer . . . very tragic—and Piers became even more withdrawn after that. Buried himself in his books, bottling everything up inside him. It hit him very hard, his mother's death.' Her mouth tightened. 'I dare say it affected Hugo, too—maybe it had something to do with him going off the rails the way he did, though he was always wild. Led his father a terrible dance sometimes, though of course that was nothing compared with later . . . Best forgotten, all that.'

She shook her head as though to rid it of some unwelcome memories. 'I usually break for coffee around eleven,' she told Cressida, changing the subject deliberately, 'and Sir Piers has his lunch at one. I'll get yours at the same time, shall I?'

'And I'll eat in here,' Cressida affirmed. 'Oh—and thank you very much for the marvellous dinner last night. It really was delicious.'

A smile of pleasure spread over Mary's face.

'I enjoyed doing it,' she confessed. 'It's been—oh—months, since Sir Piers entertained anybody, and it was quite a treat to get the silver out and make an occasion of it.'

Cressida imagined, from what she had heard, that there had been a lot more social life in his brother's time.

'Did you work here for Sir Hugo?' she asked, following Mary out into the corridor.

'No.'

The harshness of the abrupt reply told Cressida a lot. No love had been lost between Sir Hugo and the local community.

'I came when Sir Piers inherited the Priory,' Mary continued in a normal tone. 'I can just about manage on my own, but I dare say it'll be different once the visitors start coming. More dust and dirt, for a start.'

'That's something we'll have to sort out,' Cressida told her. 'But I'll need your advice on a lot of other things, too—if you don't mind, that is?'

The two women looked at one another. Cressida felt this was a crucial moment in their relationship. This was Mary's territory, and she might quite naturally feel possessive about the man and the building. It was vital to tread carefully if she were to gain the older woman's trust and ensure her help and friendship too. To her relief she saw an approving smile light up Mary's face.

'I'll be glad to help you in whatever way I can,' she said. 'Just ask, and we'll try to sort it out.'

'Thanks.'

Cressida's heartfelt gratitude must have shown on her face, for Mary leant forward and put her hand on her arm. 'You'll be fine, love—don't worry.' With that she turned and disappeared up the stairs. 'Don't forget,' she called down, 'coffee at eleven.'

Cressida felt cheered. She was sure she and Mary would get on, and at least she was assured of company for part of the day and a sympathetic ear for any troubles which might—and probably would—come her way.

And now for Sir Piers. There was a lot to be discussed before she could leave him in peace and get on on her own, and she just hoped she would find him in the right frame of mind . . . if she could find him at all, that was. Where would he be at this time of day? Better try the study first.

The door was shut, so she knocked gently, trying to get her thoughts into some sort of order. The last thing she wanted to do was irritate him by being woolly-minded at this early stage.

'Come in.'

Cressida took a deep breath and turned the handle. Yesterday had just been the overture—now the play was starting in earnest.'

Sir Piers was sitting at his desk, writing, but he stood up as Cressida came in and smiled, an easy, natural smile which lit his severe features, leaving no trace of the stiff wariness of the day before.

'Good morning. I hope you slept well?' he enquired

courteously.

'Very well, thank you. And I've had breakfast and met Mary Bryant, so I'm beginning to feel quite settled.'

Sir Piers sat down again and motioned to her to do the same. He rested his hands on the desk in front of him—no sign of the nervous finger-tattoo, and no leaping up to stare longingly out of the window. For the first time since Cressida had met him, he seemed quite at ease. She must make quite sure she said nothing out of turn to make him retreat into his shell again.

'You said there were things you needed to discuss with me?' The dark brows drew together for a moment. 'Before you begin, however, I must apologise for my manner yesterday. I fear I must have seemed very rude and dismissive.' His fingers traced the pattern in the grain of the wood, but the grey eyes held her gaze resolutely.

'I shouldn't have allowed my personal feelings to get in the way of ordinary politeness,' Sir Piers continued. 'After all, I did ask you to come here to do a job for me—I should at least have made you feel welcome.'

'But you did,' Cressida protested. 'The evening was most enjoyable, and the dinner was a great treat.' She leant forward to stress the sincerity of what she was saying. 'I do understand how disagreeable all this must be . . . no one would want strangers coming in and wandering all over their home. I know I wouldn't—and I'm sure once we sort out the practical side of things, I won't have to bother you at all.' She paused, uncertainly. 'I suppose you're absolutely determined not to take any part in whatever scheme . . .'

'No. Absolutely not.'

The shutters slammed down again, making Cressida wish she had kept her mouth shut. Stupid, she cursed herself, stupid, stupid, to upset the applecart just when he had begun to unbend.

She stretched out her hand towards him in mute apology. 'I'm sorry,' she said quietly. 'I won't mention it again, I promise.'

Sir Piers' mouth tightened as he pushed a pad of paper towards her.

'I expect you'll need this,' he said shortly. 'And a pen?' He took a ballpoint out of the tray on the desk and held it out to her.

Cressida took it and held it poised over the paper, and, as she stared down at the virgin expanse waiting to be filled with *her* ideas and suggestions, she was suddenly overcome by a terrible awareness of her inadequacy for the job.

What was she doing here—totally inexperienced and being paid to do something for which, if she were completely honest, she had no qualifications whatever?

And on the other side of the desk sat Sir Piers, last in line of an ancient and distinguished family, waiting for her to save him and his family home from disaster. There was no way she could fulfil his expectations—she might as well pack up now and go home before it all ended in disaster for everyone.

All her self-confidence evaporated as she sat there in numb misery, and it was the turn of her own fingers to betray her nervousness as, without thinking, she began picking at a loose piece of skin at the base of her thumbnail, a habit she'd fought against all her life and to which she only reverted at times of greatest stress.

Where could she start? She began to feel quite sick as she used to before some important exam, and swallowed hard as she forced herself to look directly at her employer, trying to disguise the naked panic she knew must show only too clearly on her face. He was paying her money he couldn't really afford to come up with some ideas—she *must* say something. But what? Her mind had gone a complete blank.

'I think . . .' she began uncertainly, but before she could go on Sir Piers came unexpectedly to her rescue.

'I always panic at the sight of a blank piece of paper when I'm starting on a new book,' he said kindly as he looked at her with grave sympathy. 'I'm quite aware of your lack of experience in this sort of work, but it was the enthusiasm in your letter which made me decide to offer *you* the job.'

'Oh.' The wind had been taken quite out of her sails. So she had been quite wrong to think he must have taken on the first person who had applied for the job in order to avoid meeting more strangers than he had to. He really had taken note of her application—enough to convince him she had the qualitites he was looking for. The knowledge was immensely reassuring.

'I'm sorry,' she said with a rueful smile. 'I did suffer a moment of panic, as you saw—I suddenly felt so unprepared.'

He drew the sheets of paper towards him and wrote the words 'Clarewood Priory' in large letters across the top, then pushed them back to Cressida.

'There you are,' he said with what was almost a grin. 'It doesn't look so empty now—start making a list.'

With a rush of confidence she began writing. 'Telephone', she put down, 'typewriter', 'stationery'. Pen poised, she raised her head to meet the grey, quizzical eyes full on. Her cheeks coloured slightly. But she held her gaze and, for the first time, something like a fragile thread of mutual understanding and—even more important—respect seemed to bind them together. And there was something else, too, surely—that fleeting glint in his eyes which she had noticed the evening before when, almost unwillingly she had felt, he had instinctively responded to her femininity.

All this shot through Cressida's mind in the split second of finding his attention centred on her, and her senses quivered with a surge of expectation she had to fight to suppress. Emotional involvement was something she could not allow herself.

Doing her best to fix her own attention solely on the matter in hand, she began, 'First of all I shall need a telephone and a typewriter.'

Sir Piers got up and went over to the table in the corner.

'You can have this,' he said, pointing to a typewriter next to the word processor. 'It's electric—nothing fancy, but I think you should find it reliable. As for the telephone, I'm not quite as disorganised as you might think . . .' He smiled wryly. 'I've been in touch with British Telecom and the engineers are supposed to be coming this week to put an extension in your office.'

'Thanks.' Cressida made notes on her pad which looked much less intimidating now she had started writing on it in earnest, and took a deep breath before broaching the question to which she had been looking forward least of all.

'There's something else . . .'

'Lots of things, I should think,' Sir Piers riposted drily. 'A telephone and a typewriter won't get you very far.'

He's actually teasing me, Cressida realised in astonishment. Maybe he, too, was feeling more cheerful now the dreaded hurdle of meeting her and setting all this in motion had been safely and relatively painlessly negotiated.

'It's money, I'm afraid,' Cressida continued with a surge of resolve. 'I'll need a float of some sort—for stationery, tickets, advertisements . . . that sort of thing. I won't know till I start how much I shall need, and of course I'll do my best to be as economical as I can. I won't keep asking for more if I can possibly avoid it.'

'I'd thought of that already,' Sir Piers told her. 'I've arranged to open a special account at the nearest branch of my bank. I'll take you there later on to fix it all up.' He paused and looked across at her with a definite gleam of humour in his eyes. 'That brings me to something I should have thought was quite vital and which you haven't mentioned yet.'

Cressida stared helplessly at her notes and racked her brain, feeling very stupid and inadequate. This man, for all his apparent detachment, sometimes bordering on the positively aloof, had an uncomfortable way of bringing you up short with a glance or a comment which made you realise he was definitely in command on his own home ground, however much he claimed total uninterest in the 'visitors' scheme. The legacy of all those past generations of land-owning Aylwards lay in more than just the estate and the Priory. They had left him with an instinctive and deep-seated self-assurance which underlaid his every word and gesture. In another man it might be called arrogance, but there was nothing arrogant about Sir Piers. It was simply that he knew who he was and his place in the world.

'What about transport?' he asked, bringing her back to earth.

'Transport?' she echoed dimly.

'To get you to and from the Priory,' he explained tolerantly. 'I don't imagine you'll be able to transact all your business by telephone. And I can tell you, buses in this area are so few and far between they're practically invisible.'

'Just like back home,' Cressida agreed. 'Almost non-existent and very expensive.'

'So you'll need something else, won't you? Unless you have your own car?'

Cressida shook her head. 'No, I haven't, though I can drive.'

'Well, that's no problem then. There are two vehicles here. I call them vehicles as they are hardly grand enough to be termed "cars"—an old Land Rover and an ancient Ford dating back to my father's time. Not nearly smart enough for Hugo and his dainty wife . . .'

Cressida shot him a wary look, but he continued without any of the bitterness which had underlined his comments on his brother the day before.

'They're serviceable enough. I'll show you later and you can have a test drive.'

He rose to his feet now and took up his favourite position by the window, his body half turned away from her and his eyes firmly fixed on the parkland beyond the confines of the room.

Cressida let her own gaze dwell on the broad figure while his concentration was elsewhere. No doubt, she thought shrewdly, this sudden and unexpected rush of helpfulness on his part was merely in order to get the whole distasteful business over as soon as possible. The sooner she was launched on her plans, the sooner he could return to his book and his garden. But if only he were always like this, open and accessible, she could look forward to the job with a lot more confidence and enjoyment, too. She sighed and chewed the end of her pen before wiping it clean hurriedly on her handkerchief—it wasn't hers, she remembered, as she put it back on the desk.

The soft sound roused Sir Piers from his thoughts.

'Is there anything else?' he enquired, his eyes constantly straying through the window as though he longed to be out of doors doing something physical instead of being cooped up here.

'If I could take the typewriter?'

'Of course.'

Sir Piers strode over to the corner of the room and lifted the heavy machine with as little difficulty as he had carried her luggage the day before.

When he had it installed in her office, he stood in the middle of the floor, staring round with a slight frown before his gaze finally settled on her.

'I'm afraid it's not very grand,' he commented, his hand gesturing round at the shabby surroundings.

'It's fine, really,' Cressida hastened to reassure him. 'Once I get going, it'll be so full of paper and files, the whole room will take on an identity of its own. Bright, modern furniture would give quite the wrong sort of image, anyway, and those chairs are really comfortable.'

A look of relief spread over his face—clearly all expenditure would have to be kept to the absolute minimum, and once he had left, and she had settled down to begin drawing up some preliminary plans and getting her ideas into some sort of order, the full realisation of what he was entrusting her with started to dawn on her.

But at the same time too she began to think that she might, just, with a lot of luck, make a success of the job he had asked her to do.

Time would tell. She could only do her best.

CHAPTER FIVE

THAT day and the days that followed it went by so quickly that Cressida could hardly believe it when she realised she had been at Clarewood Priory for over a month.

She, Sir Piers and Mary Bryant had developed a good, though hardly close, working relationship which, so far as **her** employer was concerned, meant keeping out of one another's way as much as possible. They ate separately and their paths barely crossed except by accident.

But at least when they did meet, Sir Piers now always greeted her with a courtesy she wouldn't have dared hope for on that first occasion of their meeting.

'But he never asks me about my work,' Cressida confided despairingly to Mary one day over their mid-morning cup of coffee. 'I know he said that very first day that he wanted nothing to do with the visitors or my arrangements, but you'd think by now he'd be curious to know what was going on, if nothing else.'

Mary laughed. 'The Aylwards are nothing if not stubborn,' she said, 'and once they've made up their minds to something, nothing will change them. He's a proud man, Sir Piers, and it comes hard to have to admit you can't run the estate without some sort of outside help. How are you getting on, anyway?'

'I'll tell you this for nothing—I couldn't have got on as well as I have without your help. I'd have given up long ago.'

Cressida's first impressions had been proved correct. Right from the start she and Mary had got on so well that she couldn't imagine what it would have been like without her friendship to rely on.

But there was one topic which never came up between them and one which Mary clammed up on just like Sir Piers, and that was anything to do with Sir Hugo and his wife. She'd tried to make a few tentative enquires, not to be nosy, but to help fill in the background more than anything, but these had been abruptly rebuffed and Cressida had given up asking about the pair and their relationship with Sir Piers. It wasn't exactly a conspiracy of silence so much as what seemed to be a universal desire to blot out everything that had gone on here in Sir Hugo's day. Cressida had had to content herself with the few snippets of information she had gleaned that first day from Sir Piers himself.

Apart from that, Mary had proved to be a tower of strength as well as a mine of information—she knew everyone in the area for miles around and this local knowledge had been invaluable when it came to finding people to help out in so many different ways. Now she had a long list of volunteers ready and waiting to come and man the rooms when finally the Priory was opened to the public, as well as to help with car parking, sell tickets . . . half the local population seemed to be involved in one way or another, and mostly thanks to Mary Bryant.

There were still a thousand details to sort out, but at least the foundations of the scheme had been laid and at last Cressida had begun to think she could even, maybe, fix a tentative date for the opening.

'That, surely, must be cause for celebration,' Cressida ventured, 'but what kind of celebration? A bottle of plonk for you and me one lunch time?' She sighed. 'Perhaps we'd better leave it till I've broken the glad tidings to Sir Piers. His reaction might well cast a damper on our enthusiasm—he might even want to go away altogether. What do you think?'

Cressida stared unhappily at her coffee-mug, stirring it absent-mindedly with a spoon that happened to be lying on the table.

Mary smiled. She knew Cressida never took sugar.

'And you'd mind, wouldn't you—if he went away?'

The hand paused. 'It shouldn't make any difference, should it? I never see him from one day's end to the other, not if he has anything to do with it. Blast!'

Her hand had resumed its stirring with such violence that some of the coffee slopped over, and she got up to get a cloth to mop up the mess.

'It's silly, isn't it? I hardly know him, not really, and if anything, he resents me being here at all. Not that he's ever rude . . . but I feel I'm just a necessary evil to him and one which he'd rather pretend to himself is practically invisible. He's never ever asked me anything about myself. And yet . . .'

'And yet . . .?' Mary prompted, a teasing light in her eye.

'And yet, if he were to go away, the whole thing would seem rather pointless. I hardly ever see him, but I know if he's around.'

'And you'd rather share the plonk with him than with me?' Mary's sharp eyes twinkled with mischief. 'Anyone would think you have designs on him—and a title for yourself.'

'Mary Bryant!' Cressida flushed scarlet to the roots of her hair. 'I thought you were my friend. How could you think such a thing?'

Mary leant forward and patted her arm. 'Sorry, love, only teasing—it was too good a chance to miss. P'raps I went too far . . .'

She rested her elbows on the table and considered Cressida more seriously. 'Why not ask him to dinner?'

'In his own house? Hardly the done thing, is it?'

'No . . . listen. Suppose I don't come in one day. Actually, I could do with some time off, especially if we're going to be as busy as you say we are . . .'

'Let's hope,' Cressida murmured. 'Go on—this sounds interesting.'

'Well, Alan wants me to go with him to see his relatives up near King's Lynn, but whatever we decided to do, you could offer to do the cooking for Sir Piers instead of me—get him to eat supper in here instead of taking it in on a tray . . . and there you are! Bingo!'

Cressida thought for a moment and looked round at the homely surroundings.

'I could make it quite cheerful, couldn't I, with some candles and flowers . . . not too formal, or alarming . . . and he did say I was to look on the Priory as my home.'

'Did he, now?'

'Stop it, Mary, or I'll have so many hangs-ups I won't dare ask him.'

'And when's it to be, this great event?' Mary asked over her shoulder as she got up to take their mugs over to the sink. 'The sooner the better, I should say, or you might have second thoughts.'

Cressida frowned. 'What about next week, say Thursday or Friday? That will give me time to plan it, and you could stay away over the weekend if you wanted to.'

Mary said she would broach the subject when she took Sir Piers his mid-day meal.

'It's all fixed,' she told Cressida gleefully when they met at lunchtime. 'He said I was to take as long as I liked—the whole week if I needed it.'

'And will you?' Cressida helped herself to the casserole gently simmering on the stove. 'I shall have a lot to live up to—you're a geat cook.'

'I'll have to see what Alan says. And when will you ask Himself to dine with you?'

'Nearer the time, I think. I'll try to find him when he's working in the garden—he's at his most amenable when he's out of doors.'

Mary shot her a perceptive look. 'You know him better than I realised,' she commented. 'Be careful, love—we can't afford any broken hearts, not at this stage.'

'Don't worry, Mary. This will be a purely friendly gesture on my part. Ten to one he won't even come,' she said with an airy lightness that deceived neither of them.

'Hmm.' Mary's voice was sceptical, but she said nothing more, leaving Cressida to work out in her mind how she could phrase the invitation in such a way that Sir Piers would be neither irritated by the change in routine, nor frightened off. It wouldn't be easy.

It was in the late afternoon the following Wednesday that Cressida wandered out into the garden in search of her quarry. She'd tried the study first, but the door was open and the room empty. She hadn't really expected to find him there, though, for by now she had a good idea of how he spent his day—very ordered, very disciplined, keeping to the same timetable wherever possible.

On the rare occasions when she absolutely had to consult him about anything, she always found him hard at work at his book or estate business directly after breakfast. Afternoons were devoted to outside jobs, and sure enough, as she rounded the corner of the East wing, there he was, crouched down over the Elizabethan garden, bedding out some plants in the newly prepared soil.

Cressida's feet crunched on the gravel between the little geometrically laid-out beds, but he didn't look up until he had filled the small space to his satisfaction.

'It's coming on, isn't it?'

Cressida often took a walk round the gardens at the end of the day, and had observed the progress of his painstaking work with interest.

'It looks a lot different from the way it did on the day I arrived,' she acknowledged. 'You must have almost finished, haven't you?'

Sir Piers straightened up, brushing back his hair with a dirty hand which left an endearing streak across his forehead. He put his hands into the small of his back and stretched with a rueful smile.

'I must be getting old,' he complained. 'I'm quite stiff. Still . . .' He gazed critically at his handiwork, the neatly clipped hedges surrounding the intricate pattern of flower-beds filled with small, green anonymous plants which later that summer would burgeon into geraniums, begonias, marigolds and sweet-scented stocks.

'Next year I'll be better organised, and grow my own plants from seed, but for now these will have to do.'

He couldn't disguise a gleam of pride and Cressida took her chance.

'Time for a small celebration, perhaps? A double celebration, actually . . . ' Even as she said the words her voice trailed away. Now you've blown it, she berated herself. He won't want to celebrate the completion of your plans—quite the reverse, in fact. How to retrieve the situation?

She had at least gained his attention, though not at all in the way she had wanted.

'A double celebration?' he asked suspiciously. 'For what?'

The grey eyes searched her face and already she could sense an instinctive withdrawal as his body tensed as though for flight. If only he weren't so wary of her . . . if only she could reach out and touch him, reassure him that she was on his side. She forced a lightness into her voice.

'Oh, nothing special—just something that's taken a lot of time lately . . . I'm sorry, I didn't mean to mention it at all.'

The 'something' happened to be the production of a small guide-book based on the notes Sir Piers had compiled for her. Actually, she would have to get his approval for it, in spite of his determination to have nothing to do with the rest of her plans. It was his house, after all, and it was vital to check the facts before the book went off to the printers. Maybe she could ask him about it at the dinner party—if there was one.

The expression on his face softened a little, and Cressida knew that it was now or never.

'I gather Mary's going away for a couple of days,' she said casually, as though Mary's plans had had nothing whatever to do with her, 'so I wondered whether you would let me make supper for you—for us—tomorrow evening, just as a return for that lovely dinner you gave me on my first evening, and, like I said, as a celebration for finishing the Elizabethan garden.'

There, she'd done it. Gloomily she waited for his response, though she was quite sure now that he'd never accept. He'd find some excuse to hide away in his study and get his own supper as he always did—anything rather than agree to spend even part of an evening in her company.

You couldn't read anything on that face—just a slight tightening of the lips betrayed the internal struggle Cressida felt sure was going on behind the impassive features. Courtesy versus detachment—which would win?

'Thank you.' Cressida could almost feel the words being forced out. 'It's a very kind thought, and I shall be pleased to accept.'

The formality of the words made her want to giggle. Anyone would think she were inviting him to the Ritz instead of a modest meal in his own home. But she knew better than to show any of her own feelings. It must be catching, this grave impassivity—her own parents would have difficulty in recognising their outgoing, 'chuntering' daughter.

'That's good,' was all the enthusiasm she would permit herself, then, prosaically, 'Will you mind eating in the kitchen? I don't think it would be quite right for me to use the dining-room, and my office is too cluttered at present.'

'The kitchen will be fine,' Sir Piers assured her with a slow smile behind which Cressida thought she could detect a glimmer of relief. An informal meal in the kitchen would be easy to escape from once they had finished eating. No tradition of coffee and port with polite conversation attached to that kind of socialising.

Now she had achieved her aim she left him to his gardening. No point in outstaying her welcome. There would be plenty of time to try to draw him out on Thursday evening, and, if good food and wine couldn't persuade him to lower his defences just a fraction, she would give up trying on the spot and concentrate all her energies on her job. Getting through to the real man would be a lost cause.

After a consultation with Mary she had previously decided on the menu—nothing too complicated, as she could hardly be described as an expert cook and did not want any disasters, yet something which showed she had actually taken trouble over the occasion.

Avocado to start with, they had decided, followed by a chicken casserole which she had made successfully at home several times, with new potatoes and mange-tout, if she could find some in the local shops. Then an exotic ready-made sweet from a specialist delicatessen in the next town, cheese and a very expensive wine which she had been assured was just the thing for a special dinner.

Cressida spent the whole day shopping, cooking and finally, when the food was all taken care of, decorating the kitchen with flowers and candles, so that by the time she had got everything ready she felt she had worked harder than in the whole of the weeks she had been at the Priory.

If that doesn't do the trick, she thought, gazing round the room, then nothing will and I'll throw in the towel. It really looked very attractive, although a far cry from the dining-room with its silver and porcelain—or a meal on a tray in the study.

She took equal care over her own appearance, too, and from her limited wardrobe chose a pretty frilled blouse to go with the skirt she had worn for dinner on her first evening. She allowed herself one hint of frivolity in the gold, strappy sandals which she had bought for a London party and hardly ever worn since.

Cressida peered at her face framed in the bedroom mirror, touching up the make-up on her eyes and lips—but no blusher, she decided. The cooking and her heightened emotions gave her cheeks quite enough natural colour.

'Calm down,' she told herself out loud, sensing her pulses quicken at the prospect of the evening ahead. 'It's only old Sir Piers you're cooking for, not some wild first date. He won't even notice what you've got on—you know him.'

But *he* didn't know *her*, and that was what all this was about.

Her high heels clicked a terse accompaniment to her heartbeats as she went down the passage towards the study. The door was half-open and she knocked gently. Sir Piers was sitting at his desk, frowning anxiously over some papers, but he looked up as she entered, his expression lightening a little in surprise at the transformation in her appearance.

'If you'd like to come along to the kitchen in about ten minutes, Sir Piers, I think supper will be ready then.'

He stood up and looked ruefully down at his customary garb of shapeless sweater and cords.

'You've changed,' he accused her. 'You told me you were just cooking supper—you said nothing about dressing up for it.' His eyes widened slightly as they travelled slowly from her face down to her frivolous toes and back again. 'You look very festive, Miss Heaton.'

Cressida felt her cheeks glowing from the unexpected compliment. 'Thank you,' she smiled. 'I just felt like changing from my everyday clothes . . . makes it more of an occasion, somehow.' She saw his dark brows go up and went on hastily, 'I'll see you in a few minutes, then?'

Sir Piers nodded. 'It's very good of you to bother.'

'Wait till you've tasted my cooking,' Cressida countered. 'You might not think it's so good then—I can't compete with Mary.'

She turned swiftly on her golden heels and made her way to the kitchen. So far, so good. She cast a critical eye round—she had already done all the preliminary washing-up, so all the pots and pans were tidied away, leaving the work surfaces clear for the plants and flowers she had arranged. She lit the red candles on the old pine table, made a final adjustment to the table napkins and stood back to admire the effect. It all looked, in Sir Piers' words, very festive.

After exactly ten minutes he appeared in the doorway and for an awful moment, as he stopped to take in yet another transformation, Cressida thought Sir Piers might retreat, but something about her shy smile of welcome made him change his mind.

'I wasn't expecting anything like this—just an omelette, something like that.' He stared at the table, alight now with the flickering candles, then down at his shabby clothes. 'I should have changed, at least.'

'I wanted it to be a surprise,' Cressida told him, watching him anxiously. 'I thought . . . it *is* only supper, nothing at all grand, and I felt like dressing it up a bit. You don't mind, do you?'

It was a bit of a cheek, looking at it from his point of view—he might take it that she hankered after a bit more style than the meal-on-a-tray kind of meal provided as a matter of course at the Priory.

'Of course I don't mind,' Sir Piers declared, taking the glass of sherry Cressida offered him. 'In fact, I'm very flattered. And you don't have to sound so apologetic—I'm not about to run away, whatever impression I might have given you.'

'Well——' Cressida took courage from this sudden burst of honesty. 'Maybe I did rather spring it on you—I suppose it wasn't quite fair.'

'But you thought I might not have come if you told me what you were really planning.' He sighed. 'I'm not the most sociable of men, and I've got into a kind of habit of solitariness. It's hard to break after all these years.'

'I'm all the more grateful that you decided to break it

just this once. And I promise I won't spring any more surprises on you—not this evening at any rate,' Cressida grinned.

Sir Piers smiled absent-mindedly, his thoughts clearly somewhere else as he put his glass down on the table and grasped the back of the nearest chair with fingers which Cressida was depressed to see resume their nervous tattoo.

'There's something I'd like to say before we start on your excellent meal,' he began quietly. Cressida waited expectantly, not daring to look away while Sir Piers dropped his own gaze to somewhere near her feet.

'You have been very patient, Cressida, and very understanding. It can't have been easy for you to work for someone who made it plain from the outset that he wanted nothing to do with the job he was actually employing you to do.'

He turned away and went to examine some of the flowers. 'Not from the garden,' he commented to himself, touched by the discovery that she must have bought them specially.

'I imagine you must be nearly ready to announce the opening date. Was that the other half of this "double celebration" as you called it?'

'Oh, dear.' Cressida's heart sank. 'That just slipped out—I could have bitten my tongue off . . . I didn't mean to mention it at all. Please——' she stretched out her hand towards him '—let's just eat and forget my job just for this evening. Can't we pretend . . . oh, I don't know . . . that we're just friends having supper together? Talk about gardening, or something?'

The words accelerated in desperation, and for the first time Cressida actually saw his face soften in genuine concern—for her.

'Friends,' he repeated softly, as though the very word

were unfamiliar to him. He reached for his glass and raised it.

'To friendship,' he said more firmly, 'and to gardening. And,' he added with a smile, 'to the opening of Clarewood Priory.' He sipped his sherry gratefully. 'It's no use trying to hide it, Cressida. You came to do a job, you've obviously made considerable headway and of course you want to celebrate. I can't go on being a complete ostrich about it.'

He looked round at the candles and flowers, the avocados already set out on their dishes, the casserole filling the room with its tempting aroma.

'And you've gone to all this trouble, too.' He pulled out a chair and motioned Cressida towards it. 'I've talked enough—I apologise.'

It was like a repeat performance of the first evening—the conversation beginning slowly, although less stiltedly than the previous occasion, yet, under the influence of the wine that Cressida had chosen with such care, the atmosphere perceptibly warmed until she sensed he really was beginning to feel more at ease in her company than he had ever done before. If only it could always be like this.

'This is really very nice,' Sir Piers said, finishing the last of his cheese. He leant back in his chair, his long legs stretched out before him. 'Supper on a tray is all very well and convenient, but I must say, this makes a very pleasant change.' He waved a hand towards the table. 'I do appreciate it . . . especially as I know how hard you've been working.'

'I thought you didn't . . .'

'You thought I took no notice of what you were doing.' The grey eyes sought the green and held them in a quizzical gaze. 'You can't live under the same roof as someone and not be aware of what they are up to. You hear the telephone, the typewriter . . . people come and go, the car's not there when you want it . . .'

'You said I could borrow it whenever I needed it,' Cressida protested hotly.

'Exactly—and as I don't imagine you're the sort of girl who'd use it for joy-riding, you must have been using it on business.'

'You've been spying on me—that's not fair!' Cressida remonstrated with a grin.

'Not spying.' Sir Piers shook his head. 'As I said, just aware—that's all.'

He thought for a moment and added quietly, 'There's something else I'm aware of. All this time we've been talking most agreeably, but I've never asked you anything about yourself.'

He smiled at her almost shyly. It was strange for a man with the confidence that took him to the remotest parts of the world, sprung from roots firmly embedded in their own corner of England, with the self-assurance that must give him, to be so uneasy in the company of comparative strangers. Or was it only she who made him so wary?

'Maybe it's because you don't like *your* life examined under a microscope that you think everybody's the same?' Cressida suggested, hoping to draw him out now that he was beginning to relax a little. 'And there's nothing special about me at all. There's no reason why you should interest yourself in my affairs. I'm just here to do a job.'

'No.' He leant across the table, startling her by the suddenness of the movement. 'You're wrong. There's every reason. This evening, for a start. If I'd taken the trouble to get to know you better, all this wouldn't have taken me so by surprise—and you wouldn't have had to get me here under false pretences.'

'I didn't,' Cressida protested. 'All I did was ask if I could make supper instead of Mary, or to save you having to get it for yourself. There weren't any false pretences about that . . .' She met his gaze squarely and grinned. 'Maybe I just didn't tell you the whole story.'

'And what about this "double celebration"?' Sir Piers regarded her sceptically from under his dark brows, but the early suspicion seemed to have vanished, leaving only a normal curiosity.

'The Elizabethan garden, you mean . . .?'

'And?'

Cressida sighed—she might have known he wouldn't let her get away with it.

'Oh, just that I'm getting on quite well with my plans—but you don't want to know about that. I promised.'

The long fingers played idly with a crumb, rolling it round his plate.

'Maybe I've changed my mind. Don't you think I should be told what stage you've reached? Then I can plan my escape.'

It was Cressida's turn to look suspicious. Was he serious, or, incredibly, teasing her? There was only one way to find out.

'Really?' she hazarded.

'Really.' He gazed gravely at her, his expression unfathomable in the candlelight. 'It is my house,' came the light reminder.

'And *you* told *me* you wanted nothing to do with my arrangements,' Cressida countered, 'but if you're sure . . . there is something I'd like your advice about, and yes, we can fix the opening date if you're agreeable. I didn't want to risk spoiling the meal by talking about that, especially as . . .'

'Especially as you suspect I might have shut up like a

clam if you had.'

Cressida looked helplessly at him. He seemed determined to confuse her, and she wasn't at all certain which avenue he was trying to drive her down.

'You're not being fair,' she began, but he interrupted her.

'I know—I'm sorry, and don't look so worried.' He smiled at her. 'Look—I rather pride myself on my coffee. You go and collect whatever it is you need for our discussion, and I'll make the coffee and bring it along to the study. Call it my contribution to a very pleasant evening, and I do thank you very much for the thought behind it. I've enjoyed myself very much indeed.'

Cressida pushed her chair back and got to her feet.

'More than you anticipated.' She made it into a statement rather than a question, daringly looking sideways at him from under her lashes.

'Much more,' he answered solemnly. His back was turned towards her as he went to collect the coffee from the cupboard so she couldn't see the expression on his face. But from his tone she thought—she hoped—he was smiling.

CHAPTER SIX

CRESSIDA spread the typed draft of the guide-book to Clarewood on Sir Piers' desk, and sat down in one of the leather armchairs to await his arrival with the coffee, feeling rather pleased wtih herself and with life in general.

For the first time he seemed to be allowing himself to unbend—not far, not yet—but he had gone so far as to admit he had actually enjoyed himself. That was a definite start, and perhaps she could repeat the occasion now he had found being alone with her was neither frightening nor compromising.

If she could only build on the fragile foundations she had laid this evening, maybe a real friendship might develop. Cressida dared not think any further than that, but simply to be able to talk naturally to him, share the occasional evening cup of coffee—that would make life a lot more pleasant and less lonely, too, for both of them.

Watching the economical efficiency of his gestures as he placed the coffee on a table and began pouring it into the china cups carefully arranged on the tray with an antique cream jug and sugar basin, Cressida wondered how many of the Aylward ancestors would have deigned to wait on one of their employees. Recalling that succession of stern faces lining the walls of the Great Hall, she couldn't repress a smile. Not only would it never have occurred to them to do such a thing, but they would be appalled at the standards to which their descendant, Piers, had been forced to stoop.

'Something amusing you?' he enquired as he offered the tray.

'Cressida smiled. 'It just struck me that your ancestors would definitely not approve of your making and serving coffee to me in this way.' She poured some cream into the delicate cup and swirled it round with her spoon.

'Not quite the thing at all,' Sir Piers agreed lightly. Then he sighed. 'But I dare say there's a lot they wouldn't approve of, especially letting the public into the Priory.'

He leant his broad shoulders against the mantelpiece, stirring his own cup slowly, and Cressida was again forcibly struck by the extraordinary family likeness which ran through each succeeding generation: the straightness of the nose, the firm chin and dark brows which contrasted so markedly with the smooth fair hair and grey eyes. She wondered which far off Aylward had been born with the strong genes passed down through the centuries.

She felt the grey eyes on her and flushed slightly as she lifted her own to meet his gaze.

'You seem preoccupied, Miss Heaton?'

At least she knew him well enough to know he only called her 'Miss Heaton' when at his least serious. He raised his cup to his lips, but his gaze never wavered.

'I was still thinking about your ancestors and wondering which one, way back, was the first to pass on those distinctive features you all have.'

'Some ancient Norseman, tradition has it—who knows?' He shrugged. Obviously the topic was of little interest to him, but Cressida's fancy ranged across the North Sea to that distant Viking chieftain adventuring along the coast in search of plunder and land until he finally settled in these parts with a local woman, most likely, founding the dynasty which only now was in danger of losing the ancestral lands the family had held so long. And she, Cressida Heaton, was the one person whom fate had elected to avert that disaster.

'Extraordinary,' she mused aloud. 'I can't imagine how it must feel to have such a direct line behind you, stretching all that way back through the centuries. It must give you such a feeling of security—and pride, too.'

Sir Piers drained his cup and put it on the table, looking down on Cressida with a wry smile.

'I don't know about that—more worry than security, I think, hoping to save the Priory and keep it up in the manner to which it—and the ancestors—have been accustomed.' His eyes slanted across to his desk. 'Which brings us to what it is you wanted to talk to me about.'

Cressida finished her own coffee and went over to the desk, her heart beating faster with trepidation. After all, this was the first time he had shown any interest in her work and it was vital that the guide-book above all should meet with his approval.

'I do hope it's all right,' she said anxiously. 'I'm no scholar, and although I stuck like a limpet to those notes you gave me, I just don't know whether I've got all the facts right. I did try very hard, and to make it interesting as well.'

Sir Piers came round to stand by her side, looking down on the spread-out sheets, the result, did he but know it, of many hours of burnt midnight oil.

'You have worked hard,' he commented with what sounded like admiration in his voice. 'And without any help from me . . .' He shook his head, frowning as his fingers riffled through the pages. 'I shouldn't have let you . . .'

A stabbing anxiety sickened Cressida as she stared at him, eyes wide with dismay. She should have summoned up her courage and persuaded Sir Piers to write it himself . . . writing was his line, after all. She couldn't bear the prospect of having to rewrite it, and there wasn't time either, not to do it properly.

'You mean it's no good?' she enquired faintly. She had so much wanted to earn his approval, and until this moment she hadn't been aware quite how much.

'Oh, no—I'm sorry . . . you misunderstand.'

Cressida looked quickly up into his face. 'You mean . . .?'

'From what I can see, it looks fine—very good, in fact. What I meant was, I shouldn't have let you do it all alone, take all the responsibility. It must have taken hours of your time over and above all your other work.'

Waves of relief swept over her. 'As long as it's all right, that's all that matters. I was so afraid you were going to say it wasn't good enough.'

Sir Piers put down the pages he had been holding. 'I'll go over it tomorrow,' he promised, 'and I'll let you know if anything needs altering, though I'm sure there won't be much. Then it can go to the printers.'

He straightened up and turned to face her directly, smiling.

'No wonder you felt like celebrating. I know what it's like when you finish a piece of writing. A kind of relieved satisfaction at a job well done—or at least you hope it's well done.'

Cressida nodded. 'I was so scared—well, I still am, a little, as you haven't actually read it yet. I thought you might think it was a load of rubbish. After all, you're a professional writer, and I've never done anything even remotely like this.'

'I think a brandy is called for, at the very least. We must baptise this new work with something worthy of the occasion.'

Sir Piers crossed over to the cupboard and brought

out a very expensive-looking bottle and two balloon glasses. 'Will you join me?'

Cressida's shoulders relaxed with relief.

'Thank you, Sir Piers.'

Not looking at her, but keeping his eyes firmly fixed on the stream of golden liquid, he said, so quietly she wasn't sure whether she heard him correctly, 'I think it's time we dropped the "Sir".' He put the bottle down carefully and held out one glass to Cressida. As she took it, their fingers touched. Recalling vividly his instinctive recoil from that first physical contact in the Hall, the day she had arrived, she made as if to step back, but, to her amazement and with a violent leap of her heart, she felt his fingers close more firmly round her own, imprisoning both them and her glass in their gentle grasp.

'Piers?'

His name only came out as a hoarse whisper as their eyes met and held.

All the emotions she had been suppressing—emotions she hadn't even been fully aware of until now—swept over her in a glorious tidal wave of elation. The whole world became pinpointed on their linked fingers and the glowing gold of the liquid mirrored in the glinting lights deep in the sea-grey depths. Every nerve in her body was arrowing towards the vital sensation of his touch on her skin and she dared not move for fear—a terrible, delicious fear—he would seize on the slightest movement as a token of her withdrawal. She knew if she let him back away into his shell it would be for ever.

How long they stood there, bound by such a fragile thread of contact, she could not have said. Time ceased to have any meaning, but she would willingly have stayed there, motionless, all night, growing ever more conscious of the tension between them.

And still those grey eyes held hers in a gaze mesmerising

in its intensity. She was unable to move, unable to respond . . . she wasn't sure what he wanted of her. If only . . . her lips ached for his, and, almost imperceptibly and of its own volition, her body swayed towards him until, with a new surge of delight, she heard Piers catch his breath.

With his free hand he took the glass and reached behind him to place it on the table, still without moving his eyes from her face, as though he were seeing it clearly for the first time, then slowly, gently, his lips at last came down to seek hers with a butterfly caress. She felt his arm slide round her waist, and with a gasp she fell against him, shyly linking her own arms round the hard, broad back.

His mouth sought hers more ardently now, and she responded gladly, matching the urgency of his embrace, almost unable to believe what was happening. This proud, reclusive man, who had kept himself so detached ever since her arrival, actually held her in his arms! She had finally achieved the impossible and demolished the icy barriers of reserve. Bubbles of joyous intoxication rose up within her until she could contain her emotions no longer, and they erupted in a happy laugh.

'Oh, Cressida!'

Piers' arms tightened round her, holding her close; then he loosened his hold a little to step back, running his hands over her shoulders and down her arms until she felt his fingers grasp her own and she met his gaze, alight with a sort of astonished joy.

'You didn't mind?'

Cressida shook her head, the dark tresses tumbling round her flushed cheeks, and for answer she lifted her face, reaching up to bring his down, gently brushing her lips against his mouth again. She felt the smooth skin of his cheek under her hand, then he caught up the hand to kiss each finger in turn before holding her palm against his lips with such tenderness in his eyes that she thought her heart would burst.

'Cressida.'

Even the way he spoke her name was a caress, as he savoured the syllables on his tongue.

'Cressida . . .?' he repeated, questioning—but what he wanted to ask was never uttered. The words were cruelly and abruptly cut off by the shrill of the telephone, the loud, intrusive noise bursting into the silence with a shocking suddenness. They looked at one another in dismay, then Cressida dropped her arms.

'Who the hell . . and at this hour, too?'

Reluctantly Piers loosed her hands and strode over to the strident machine, snatching up the receiver with irritation.

'Yes—Piers Aylward here.'

His voice was harsh. Cressida put her hands to her warm cheeks, longing for the caller to go away, for it to be a wrong number so that Piers would turn back to her and take her in his arms again before the enchantment was shattered for ever. She wrapped her own arms round her body, watching him, but the look on his face told her more clearly than any words could have done that the real world had encroached on their brief and unexpected idyll.

She took a step towards him—then stopped. She mustn't presume. The call was nothing to do with her, she could tell by the hardening of his expression, the tightening of the mouth which only moments ago had been pressed so urgently to hers.

Cressida turned away as much to hide her misery as from tact, and quietly collected their cups and put them back on the tray. She would take it back to the kitchen and leave Piers to transact whatever unpleasant business had so suddenly confronted him. But before she had reached the door she saw him beckoning to her to stay where she was.

'I see,' Piers said shortly to the unwelcome caller. 'And there's no alternative? No, no—not here!' He glanced quickly over to Cressida, then let his eyes fall back on to the papers on his desk which he pushed round absent-mindedly with his free hand.

'No—I'll come . . . tomorrow. It's most inconvenient, but if that's the only way . . .'

Something else was said which touched his face with a bleakness so hopeless that it made Cressida want to rush forward and enfold him in her arms, but she gripped her hands tightly together and waited quietly for him to finish the call and put the phone down.

Piers walked slowly back to the centre of the room, hands by his sides now, making no attempt to reach out to her. The spell was broken.

'I'm sorry,' Cressida began. 'Is there anything I can do?'

A bitter smile twisted the taut lines of his features which not so many minutes before had been smoothed into softer contours.

'Nothing,' came the sharp reply, then, seeing the hurt in the green eyes wide with concern, he touched her briefly on the arm.

'A private matter—disagreeable, and very badly timed.' He went quickly over to the corner of the room and retrieved the brandy glasses, one of which he held out to Cressida. The other he raised to his lips and drained in one gulp.

'Not quite the celebration we had in mind.' He gave a short laugh. 'I've got to go to London tomorrow—early. You'll be all right here on your own, won't you? Oh—and I'll take your guide-book with me. It'll give me something to read on the train.'

Cressida stared at him helplessly. To be in his arms only moments ago, only to be dismissed so casually with no reference to what had occurred between them was almost too much to bear. Surely he had felt something for her just now? The way he had murmured her name, the look on his face . . . She stared at him, hoping at least he would make a move to kiss her goodnight, but there was no warmth in the grey eyes now, only what looked like a faint irritation at her continued presence when he clearly wanted to prepare himself for whatever disagreeable meeting awaited him the next day.

The bleakness in his expression communicated itself to hers, and if he noticed the light go from her eyes he gave no sign.

'I'll leave you, then,' she offered, putting her untasted brandy down on the table beside him. 'I hope . . . I hope tomorrow goes better than you think.'

Piers uttered a non-committal grunt, but made no further acknowledgement of her concern for him.

'Fine.' Was that relief in his voice? 'I may be back tomorrow evening—it depends . . .' He raised his hand resignedly. 'Oh, and thank you again for the supper. It was a very pleasant occasion.'

How could he wipe all memory of their closeness from his mind so completely? It was as though an 'erase' button had been pressed the instant he'd lifted the receiver, which had blotted out everything that had just happened, restoring their relationship to the cautious wariness—on both sides—she had taken such pains to transform.

She had invested such hopes in this evening, and now the barriers he had erected between them were back in place as though that embrace had never removed them. Her womanly instincts told her he had felt something for her, Cressida, as a person; he had found her attractive, even desirable, and who knew what that first kiss might have led to, if only . . .

No, Cressida chided herself miserably. 'If only' is a cul-de-sac and there is no point in letting your thoughts and desires go down that path. Keep your distance and maybe, one day, Piers might trust you enough to unleash his feelings once again, but there is no point in dwelling on what might have been. It would be so fatally easy to fall head over heels in love with this difficult, inaccessible man, but she must, to keep her sanity, do her utmost to pull herself back from the brink.

Cressida fell into an uneasy sleep after long, wakeful hours during which she relived every second of their embrace, still experiencing the sensation of that hard-muscled body pressed against hers, his lips on her mouth, seeking . . . seeking . . .

She awoke with a start, the events of the previous evening tumbling into her brain in a confused jumble of images—the glowing liquid in the glass, their linked hands . . . the jarring stridency of the telephone.

And she was alone. Piers would have left hours ago, she knew, but at least the solitude would give her a chance to get her thoughts into some sort of order.

She lay in bed staring up at the ceiling, the only sound the chirping of sparrows outside the window. No point in brooding—she would use the day to finalise as many of her arrangements as she could, so that at least the decks would be cleared should Piers need her assistance on his return, though it was more than likely that he would shoulder any new burdens alone. Her own job was clearly defined and she knew him well enough to realise he welcomed no outside interference, however sympathetically offered. He was a loner, and the sooner she took that fact on board once and for all, the less torment it would cause her.

She got dressed slowly, wondering where Piers was now, and what he was doing. Who had that unwelcome caller been, and what new worries were waiting to confront him? If only she could help.

The silence which pervaded the whole building seemed almost uncanny that morning, as if the very walls were waiting for Piers to return with yet another blow to their security. As she had so often at the beginning, she almost felt she should walk on tiptoe, and to counteract her superstitious imaginings she turned her portable radio up loud as she made her usual coffee and toast breakfast, clearing a corner of the table of last night's debris to make room for her plate and mug.

Her fingers couldn't help straying towards the wineglass Piers had drunk from, and with a guilty look round, although she knew full well there was no one to watch, she raised it quickly to her lips and held it there for a moment.

'I'm getting sentimental,' she said out loud to break the silence. 'Get on, girl—there's all this to tidy up. Stop mooning round like a star-struck teenager.'

The radio was blaring out the current number one pop tune, so she did not hear the postman knock at the scullery door. There was no letter-box in the great main door of the Priory and he had got into the habit of bringing the post round to the back where he could put it inside—and have a cup of tea if Mary was in the kitchen when he arrived.

'Anyone about?'

'Oh, goodness—Mr Leggate! You did make me jump!'

'I'm not surprised, with that thing blaring out!'

Bill Leggate held out a pile of letters and Cressida took them and put them on the dresser.

'On your own, aren't you? I know Mary and Alan are away visiting, and I saw the Land Rover go through the village early on.'

Cressida nodded. 'Sir Piers has had to go to London.'

'How's it going, then? When will we see all those hordes of visitors we've been promised? Best thing to happen to the village for years, if it's a success.'

Cressida's spirits lifted. Here at least was someone on her side.

'Let's keep our fingers crossed—it's all going according to plan at the moment, anyway. Mrs Tomlinson at the Post Office told me several people want to do teas, and I noticed she already has some local pottery nestling among her fruit and veg. And talking of teas, can I get you a cup? It'd be no trouble.'

Bill Leggate shook his head. 'No, thanks, love. I've got a bit behind this morning, and it's my lad's school sports day, so I want to be home in good time.'

On his way out he nodded towards the still laden table. 'You've got a lot of washing-up there.'

Cressida grinned. 'You know how it is when you're on your own. You let it all mount up and do it when you've run out of plates. Don't tell Mary, will you?'

'Go on.' Bill Leggate tapped his nose, laughing. 'Looks more like a party to me—when the cat's away . . . trust me, I'll keep mum.'

'It wasn't anything like that,' Cressida replied, taking mock offence at the very suggestion. 'All very proper, I can promise you.'

'I know, love.' He opened the door, then turned back. 'Take care, now, won't you? Look after yourself.'

With a cheerful smile he closed the door after him. What a nice man he was, Cressida thought. Some people might resent her presence here and her plans to bring in as many tourists to this peaceful Suffolk backwater as she could, but from the start he had always shown interest in her ideas, and had even suggested several people to help her.

Thinking about Bill Leggate reminded Cressida of the question which until last evening had been uppermost in her mind—the date of opening. She'd never had the chance to discuss it with Piers—it would have to be tackled when he got back, because it was now getting rather urgent. She would have to choose her moment carefully, though, as she doubted whether he would be in the most receptive of moods when he did return, judging from the expression on his face as he'd taken the call.

She drained the last of her coffee and began gathering up the plates and glasses to stack them in the dishwasher. She wondered whose idea it had been to buy it . . . Hugo's, probably, or his wife's. Piers' solitary meals would hardly justify the expense, especially as money was so tight.

She glanced casually at the pile of letters Bill Leggate had brought her. Nothing special, by the look of it. She'd deal with them later when she got the kitchen tidied up. This took quite a while, but eventually Cressida had everything put away in its proper place, and she could concentrate on her real job again. She picked up the post and carried it back to her office, pausing briefly on the way to glance in at Piers' study.

She hesitated on the threshold and the sight of the two brandy glasses still on the table brought back the events of the evening before with a vivid poignancy even last night's dishes hadn't aroused.

It had all happened so unexpectedly—had it meant anything to him at all, she wondered for the hundredth time, that embrace here, on this very spot?

Cressida closed her eyes, trying to conjure up a vision

of Piers with that expression of dawning happiness on his face which the telephone call had so abruptly removed. Surely those had been his real feelings she had glimpsed then, and if the miracle could happen once, why not again? She sighed. It was so difficult, if not impossible, to guess what went on behind that enigmatic exterior.

She walked over to the desk and started to sort through the mail, leaving thc lcttcrs addressed to Piers in a neat pile for him to deal with on his return.

Three for her, two for Piers, another for her . . . and what was this? The room reeled round and she clutched on to the edge of the desk for support. Surely she was mistaken—it couldn't be! But the writing on the envelope was uncompromising in its clarity:

Lady Aylward
Clarewood Priory,
Clarewood, Suffolk.

Lady Aylward! Oh, no . . . please, not that . . . Cressida groped for the nearest chair and fell into it, clutching the envelope in her hand, one stark fact blotting out everything else: Piers had a wife.

Why had no one thought to tell her? Who was she, and where had she been all this time? Questions she had no means of answering thundered through her brain while she did her best to come to terms with the completely altered circumstances she now found herself in.

She stared hopelessly at the letter as if it held the clue to the cruel puzzle—it bore a London postmark which told her nothing—except . . . London! The telephone call! Of course—it all began to fall into place.

Supposing Piers and his wife were estranged, seperated—divorced, even. There was a crumb of comfort in that last thought, but Cressida ignored it in her desperate search for the truth. That would at any rate account for his reclusiveness, his solitary travelling, although . . . He'd told her he had begun that when his brother had inherited the Priory, but that would have been no life for a married man, would it? Maybe his wife had grown tired of waiting for him to return from his constant travels and left him.

So why was she coming back here? For, if she weren't planning to do just that, why would the letter have been sent to this address?

Cressida's eyes strayed towards the telephone—at least she knew now who had been making that call.

Miserably she rehearsed in her mind the scene which had taken place in this room only . . . how long ago? Not more than twelve hours. Piers' tentative embrace—fearful of being repulsed when no doubt he had every reason to be wary of women after the misery of separating from his wife. No wonder he wanted nothing to do with her, Cressida, and her plans for the Priory. It wasn't only that family pride urged him to keep his distance—it was the memory of the past hurt and fear of being let down yet again. She could see it all only too plainly.

Then, just as he was beginning to feel he might be able to trust her—the telephone call. With painful vividness she saw again the bleak expression in his eyes which had flicked towards her with the words: 'No, no—not here,' and later, 'I'll come—if that's the only way.'

His wife wanted to see him again—but if only she had been forewarned . . . She suddenly heard Mary's voice the day they had planned the dinner party. What had she said?

'We can't afford any broken hearts . . .' Could it have been 'any *more* broken hearts'? She couldn't remember

—her thoughts were in such a turmoil by now—but did it really matter?

There was only one thing that mattered, the one stark, incontrovertible fact that Piers had a wife, and, until she knew whether they were still married or not, she must put him out of her thoughts—and out of her heart.

At least it hadn't got any further than one kiss . . . Cressida's gazc fell on the white square of paper in her hand, but the writing gave nothing away, and her eyes drifted over to the corner of the room where the brandy glasses still sat on Piers' table.

She *must* pull herself together . . . at least she could do something practical to remove those mute reminders of what might have been. She got quickly to her feet, replaced the fateful letter on the desk and almost ran to the kitchen with the glasses—no sentimental caress for the place where his lips had rested or their hands had touched. A hasty rinse and a wipe and they were back out of sight and out of mind.

Cressida worked herself into a frenzy that day in a determined almost manic effort to bury all images of the evening before in the very depths of her memory. She must not let Piers' private life prevent her from making a success of what she had come to the Priory to do. She even made time to write a brief note to her parents.

'Everything is going well,' she told them, with a bitter private smile. 'I've got all the publicity organised now—keep a look out in *Country Life* next month, there's a small piece on the Priory with a picture of Sir Piers. As you will see, my idea of the pipe-smoking, tweedy gent was a bit misplaced! They've promised to do a bigger feature later on, so keep your eyes peeled.'

She sucked her pen reminiscently. In the face of his stubborn determination to keep in the background and out of any publicity, it had taken all her diplomatic skills to persuade Piers to let her use his photograph, but in the end he had agreed, though only on the proviso that it was taken in the garden. The garden . . . she forced her attention back to the letter.

'Sir Piers is studying the guide-book—written by me!—and with any luck if will be off to the printers next week, and then we can decide when to open. After that, all we need is people.'

She finished her letter, put it in an envelope, licked and stamped it. Now what could she do? She got up and began prowling restlessly round. There was nothing she could see that claimed her attention and there was still no sign of Piers. She must keep busy and her mind off that other letter with all its implications.

Almost without thinking, she set off on a tour of the house, taking the vistors' route round the rooms. Anxiously she did her best to look at them with an objective eye, though it was difficult when she was so involved with it all. Was there enough here to attract visitors without a great historical name to lure the public? The people from the East Anglian Tourist Board and the team from *Country Life* had been encouraging, and there were the ruins and gardens as added attractions. She must somehow extract a promise from Piers that the Elizabethan garden would be included in the tour.

What was it he had said? 'I shouldn't have let you do it on your own.' Well, she would be lucky now if he offered any help at all—the meeting in London would only have stiffened his resolve to keep himself to himself.

Disconsolately Cressida wandered through the empty, silent rooms, and not even the South Gallery had the power to lift her spirits today. She knew that nothing would, until Piers came back and she got the true explanation of the letter addressed to his wife.

At the top of the back stairs she glanced along the passage to Piers' bedroom. Supposing . . . no, she couldn't . . . but it would put her mind at rest, for surely, if his wife were still important to him, that was where he would keep a photograph of her. There was certainly no memento of her in the study, but a bedroom—that was private territory, and knowing Piers' passion for privacy where his own life was concerned . . . She would only take a peep, but she had to know.

Her heart began thumping as she made her way along the passage quickly and silently, as though someone might find her out. The knob turned slowly under her hand, and she pushed the door open to reveal a room as orderly and uncluttered as the study. All was scrupulously tidy, with nothing more personal visible than a pair of silver-backed hairbrushes laid neatly on the tall mahogany chest of drawers.

There was a bed—single, she noted—a wardrobe, a couple of chairs, but no ornaments, no pictures, and only a few books on the bedside-table. Certainly no photographs of anyone, let alone a wife.

Her question hadn't been answered, but that room was hardly that of a happily married man who wanted constant reminders of a beloved wife.

So where had she been, this Lady Aylward, and why had everyone kept a conspiracy of silence about her very existence if she mattered so little to him?

There was no answer here, and she doubted whether even when Piers returned she would easily get to the bottom of the truth she so wanted to be told.

CHAPTER SEVEN

PIERS did not come back that day, nor the day after, either, and it wasn't until early on the Sunday evening that from her office Cressida heard the unmistakable sound of the Land Rover coming up the drive.

She went out into the passage and watched from the window which overlooked the courtyard. Grim-faced, Piers leapt out and strode straight up to the house. She heard the great main door slam to, the sound echoing through the building, and then his footsteps as they hurried to the study. Another slam, and the silence flooded back, making her feel almost more alone than she had all weekend.

Now what was she to do? She waited, nervously apprehensive—what would his reaction be to the letter? Would he come and find her, offer an explantion? He must realise she would have seen it.

Minutes passed and still there was no sound. She couldn't stay here for ever . . . she must see what was happening.

Cressida left her office and walked slowly towards the study where she stood, listening, outside the door, but she could hear no sound, no movement—nothing. It was as though Piers had never returned. Her hand lifted to knock, but something held her back. It would be better to wait . . she would see him later, when he had had time to recover from whatever it was that had etched those new lines on his face.

She cooked, ate and washed up her supper, and still

there was no sign of Piers. By now her concern for him was rapidly turning to annoyance. Even if that embrace—by now almost receding to fantasy-land—had meant nothing to him, mere courtesy should surely have made him want to find out at least whether she was all right. For all he knew or seemed to care she could be ill in bed, collapsed with a broken leg out on the estate . . . anything. No wonder Lady Aylward had left him if that was the way in which he had treated her. She had all Cressida's sympathy.

This is ridiculous, she told herself finally—I have to see him. She went back and listened again outside the door—still no sound. She plucked up her courage and knocked firmly.

'Come in.'

Piers was sitting at the desk, chin resting on his hand and staring at some papers in front of him with that old bleak look back in his eyes.

'Oh . . . Cressida.'

Who did you expect? The tart reply sprang to her lips but she bit back the words merely to ask briskly, 'I'm making some coffee and I wondered whether you would like a cup—or anything to eat?'

If it was only as his employee that he now chose to see her, then as her employer she would treat him. Nothing else.

Piers pushed the papers away from him with an irritable gesture and arranged them in a pile.

'That would be very welcome,' he said. 'Just the coffee, thanks. I don't feel very hungry at the moment.'

'Shall I bring it here?'

He nodded. 'If you don't mind.'

Cressida paused by the door. 'You . . . you got your post all right? I left all your mail on your desk.'

'Yes, thanks. Oh——'

Cressida waited, her pulses quickening. Now he would say something, surely?

'I've read your drafted guide-book. It seems first-class.' The faintest glimmer of a smile replaced the drawn look just for an instant. 'There are only one or two minor suggestions I have to make. Maybe we could go over them tomorrow morning, then take it to the printers together, if you're agreeable?'

And that was all. No reference to his trip to London, to the letter, to his wife, or to what had happened between them . . . nothing. It was as though they were right back to the beginning again.

After another restless night it seemed to be business as usual. Mary wasn't due back until the following day, for which Cressida was grateful. The last thing she felt like was having to answer all her friend's questions about the dinner party, at least not until she had found out the answers to the questions burning in her mind, and it was in a very dispirited mood that she made her way to the study to discuss the alterations Piers wanted to make to the guide-book.

'I thought we ought to keep it simple,' she explained, trying to keep her mind from straying from the job in hand. That way it will be cheaper and easier to produce,' she went on doggedly. She told him what she and the printers had in mind, 'And then if the scheme takes off in a big way, we can smarten it up, added photographs and so on, as well as provide more in the way of attractions here at the Priory, such as a tea-room and a souvenir shop.'

Piers frowned and turned away to look out of the window.

I don't know whether I like the sound of that.'

Cressida felt like shaking him. How could he be so stubborn and unhelpful? By his own account he needed the money desperately to save the Priory, but didn't seem in the least inclined to co-operate in the very plans which were the most lucrative.

'Well, we can see about that later,' she returned. 'I'll take these notes off now and put in the changes.' She walked quickly over to the door. 'You did say something about going to the printers together? If it's not convenient, I can easily go by myself—it'll be no trouble.'

If Piers was surprised by her cool and super-efficient attitude, he gave no sign.

'No, I think I'd like to go too. Just tell me when you want to go, and I'll be ready.'

It wasn't until midday that Cressida finished typing in the alterations. Piers wasn't in the study when she went to find him, so she went outside where she discovered him dead-heading pansies in the Elizabethan garden.

'I've finished now, so I could get lunch as Mary's away, and we could go to the printers afterwards.'

Working in the garden must have helped Piers to come to terms with the new problem he had brought back from London with him, for the tense lines had been smoothed away, temporarily at least, and he looked almost cheerful as he stepped carefully over the low lavender hedge, his hand full of crushed yellow and purple petals.

'I've got a better idea,' he said. 'Give me a minute or two to tidy up, and we'll go out for lunch somewhere. It's about time you saw something of the countryside, and I ought to make it up to you for the other evening—our celebration was rather cut short, and I never had time to thank you properly.'

Cressida stared at him open-mouthed. He really was the most extraordinary man. She might have found his unpredictability comically attractive—a challenge certainly—if it hadn't the power to hurt her so much, but he seemed not to find anything out of the ordinary about his proposal and stood watching her, obviously anticipating her ready acquiescence.

Cressida met his gaze coolly.

'That would be very nice,' she accepted with no great show of enthusiasm. 'I'll go and get everything together.'

What else could she do? After all, he was her boss and she could hardly plead a prior engagement. But inwardly she was seething. It had been difficult enough in the beginning, when he had barely so much as acknowledged her existence as well as making it quite plain that the less he had to do with her plans, and by implication with her too, the better, in spite of the fact that it was by his invitation and for salary he was paying her that she was here at all.

She was beginning to think that it had only been the influence of the wine and the unaccustomed comfort of the shared meal which had moved him to take her in his arms the other evening. She had merely been a convenient—and willing—outlet for instinctive desires repressed by the hermit-like existence he led.

And now, after his visit to his wife, he was naturally eager to put the whole episode from his mind and revert to his initial attitude of reserved detachment. Maybe Lady Aylward had forced some sort of confession out of him, though there was little enough to confess to in all conscience, only a kiss and a brief embrace. Nothing to compromise either of them—the interruption of the telephone had seen to that.

Even so . . . if only she could *know* how he felt. That dawning light of recognition in his eyes, the tenderness in his voice as he had murmured her name—they hadn't been feigned, surely?

So why hadn't he trusted her enough to tell her about his wife, wherever she was and whatever she had done to him? If he thought he only had to invite her out to a pub lunch for all to be forgiven and forgotten, he had another think coming, Cressida thought angrily as she collected up all the papers she needed for the visit to the printers.

Piers looked at his watch as she came into the courtyard to join him by the car.

'Lunch first, do you think? If we leave it too late, all the best places will be full up.'

'Whatever you think is best.'

Cressida climbed into the passenger seat of the old Ford and slammed the door to, arranging the folds of her cotton skirt round her knees. Actually, in spite of her ambiguous feelings about Piers, the hurt and the anger, she was looking forward to this outing— nothing very special, but at least she would see something of the world outside the Priory gates. On her previous trips she had been so intent on not getting lost in the unfamiliar countryside, and on concentrating on the people she needed to see, that she had barely taken note of her surroundings. It was different being a passenger, and she also had to admit that she was curious to see what sort of a driver Piers was. You could tell a lot about a man by the way he handled a car . . . not that he could go very fast in this clapped-out old heap.

'Any preference about where you'd like to go?' Piers enquired, swinging the car out of the gates. Why was he being so considerate all of a sudden? Was it his way of trying to make amends for the offhand manner in which he had treated her on his return from London? If so, he wasn't going to have it all his own way.

'I don't mind. Anywhere you like,' Cressida returned in a disinterested tone, keeping her eyes resolutely fixed on the passing fields and hedgerows so that she didn't notice the tightening of the knuckles on the steering-wheel, the narrowing of the grey eyes at her patent rebuff.

'If you'd rather not . . .'

'No, I'm looking forward to it,' Cressida replied with forced brightness. 'As you said, it will be nice to see something of Suffolk. Good for business, too, when visitors ask me questions about the locality.'

The car was the one to suffer from her lack of enthusiasm. Cressida winced at the crash of the gear-change, the stamp on the brakes as they came to the main road. Piers signalled right and turned in the direction of the coast, barely uttering another word until he drew up outside a neat, white pub pretty with climbing roses and with a garden signposted to the rear.

'This used to be good,' he announced briefly, turning off the engine.

When you came with your wife, Cressida was on the point of retorting, but forced a wan smile as she climbed out into the warm June sunshine.

'Shall we sit outside?' she ventured. 'It's really warm today.' She spent most of her working day indoors, and a chance to sit and relax in the open air suddenly seemed very attractive.

Piers nodded. 'As you like. You find somewhere to sit, and I'll go and get the menu. What would you like to drink?'

Cressida said she would like a white wine and went to sit down at a wooden table in a pleasant, secluded corner surrounded by pots, urns and hanging baskets, a riot of colour and scent which on a normal day would be guaranteed to lift the spirits.

But, unlike the previous occasions on which they had eaten together, the conversation did not flower with the progress of the meal. Talk ranged in a desultory fashion from the guide-book to the surroundings, and Piers told her a little about the towns and villages nearby, but gradually their fitful conversation lapsed altogether and they finished their meal in an uncomfortable silence. Cressida simply could not bring herself to respond to Piers' efforts at communication until she knew about Lady Aylward and his current relationship with her. She wasn't one of those carefree girls who didn't mind whether a man were married or not—she had been brought up in a happy home with an inborn respect for the institution of marriage, and in her heart of hearts she would have thought Piers' standards of morality would have equalled her own. And she was too proud to ask him directly.

'Would you like anything else?' Piers enquired finally, with an effort. 'Or shall we go to the printers now?'

Cressida paled before the coldness in his voice. His efforts at hospitality had been spurned, and he certainly did not intend to put himself out for her any further. She had hurt him, she knew . . . perhaps the only thing to do was to bring the whole question of his marriage into the open—now. Otherwise, there would cease to be any rapport between them at all and it would become impossible to do her job, let alone co-exist equably under the same roof.

She glanced across at him—he was still waiting for an answer to his last question, stiff and motionless, not betraying by so much as a twitch of a muscle what was going through his mind. This was not the time, quite definitely.

'I've had plenty, thanks. It was very nice.'

Piers got to his feet, pushed back his chair with an irritable movement and set off for the car without another word or a backward glance to see whether she were following. Only an almost imperceptible sag of the broad shoulders gave some indication of his innermost feelings. Disappointment at the failure of his sociable gesture in inviting her out to lunch? Depression at some unpleasant memory? Who could tell? He certainly wasn't going to.

In silence they drove to the printers where they conducted their business with the least possible mutal discussion, making all their comments and suggestions through the manager, Mr Prentice, who, if he noticed anything odd, was far too polite to let it affect his dealings with them.

He promised to have the guide-books ready in a fortnight. 'I can't see there'll be any difficulty about that—they're more leaflets, aren't they? Not actual books, no pictures or photographs to complicate matters, although Miss Heaton did tell me that if the scheme is a success, she'll hope to produce something a bit more elaborate.' He smiled from one to the other. 'I gather from your phone call that you're hoping to open in a month or so?'

Cressida nodded with a lurch of the stomach. Now the cat was out of the bag—she should have told Piers herself, not kept putting it off. And it was so soon . . . only a month!

Mr Prentice beamed at Piers. 'Well all hope it's a great success, sir—and I'll be along there with the family, you can be sure of that.'

Cressida cringed inwardly, knowing that was the last thing Piers would want to hear. She glanced anxiously at him standing stony-faced by her side, then smiled brightly at Mr Prentice.

'We'll look forward to seeing you at the Priory, Mr Prentice—and to seeing the guide-book in print. You'll let me know when it's ready, won't you, then I can come and collect it? It will be quite exciting for me, actually—I've never seen my words in print before!'

'You wrote it yourself, did you, Miss Heaton?' Mr Prentice asked in evident surprise. 'I'd have thought Sir Piers . . .'

'Oh, he's too busy on his new book—he left it all to me,' she returned quickly. 'So if there are any mistakes, it'll be all my fault.'

She edged towards the door, hoping to escape before either of them said anything to upset Piers further.

'I don't think there's anything else we need discuss, is there?'

'If there are any problems, I know where to find you.' Mr Prentice reached the door first and held it open for them. Piers nodded curtly and after a brief farewell strode out to the car.

Mr Prentice looked after him sympathetically.

'Can't be easy for him, having to open up the Priory. I know I wouldn't like it.' He sighed. 'He's had a lot to put up with over the years . . .'

He took a breath as though to expand on the subject, thought better of it and after a few more polite remarks returned to his office.

Cressida walked thoughtfully out to rejoin Piers, who was already sitting in the car waiting to drive off. What troubles was Mr Prentice referring to? Merely Hugo and the financial crisis, or a messy divorce—some sort of scandal? Was she growing over-suspicious about Piers' private affairs?

She climbed in beside him and shut the door.

'I'm sorry Mr Prentice let out the information about the opening date. I only mentioned it tentatively to him to make sure the guide-books arrived on time. I was going to discuss it with you . . . ask your opinion, that is . . .'

she swallowed hard 'the other evening . . .'

She looked across at him nervously, expecting him to erupt—that had been a tactless slip-up on her part, although she had not exactly had a lot of opportunity to raise the subject in the past few days. Still, she wouldn't blame him if he were cross.

But he wouldn't show his anger, would he? That wasn't his way. He would just drive quickly home and shut himself away behind the barriers again.

She waited. Like Mr Prentice, he seemed on the verge of saying something, but changed his mind as he turned the ignition and eased the car out of the printers' yard on to the main road.

To Cressida's surprise he did not turn the way she expected in the direction of Clarewood and the Priory, but set off down a road signposted to Dunwich which she knew was on the coast, quite unfamiliar territory as far as she was concerned. He didn't offer any explanation or say where they were going, so after a while Cressida gave up trying to fathom out what was in his mind, and decided just to enjoy the ride.

She had never been to East Anglia before this summer, but whatever preconceived notions she had had about its being dull and featureless had already been dispelled on her journeys round Clarewood. Now, as Piers drove along the narrow, high-banked lanes between green hedges and wide, fertile fields, her spirits lifted with each fresh discovery in this unspoiled corner of England. For some reason, she had always thought of it as flat and treeless, but she soon found out how wrong she had been as with every turn in the road she discovered another gentle vista of meadows, woods and little streams under the wide expanse of sky. Every now and then they would go through a village with winding streets between ancient white or colour-washed houses, half-timbered, some of them, and looking as though they had been rooted there since time immemorial.

Each farmhouse and each church had its own distinct character, and Cressida would have liked to have stopped at several places to explore and find out more, but Piers drove straight on, hardly looking at the surrounding countryside.

The wide fields and hedges gradually changed to more open country—heathlands interspersed with stands of conifers, wilder-looking than anything Cressida had seen so far. She thought they were heading towards the sea, but before she had a chance to find out Piers pulled over on to a stretch of grass, wiry and tough, scattered with gorse-bushes and bracken. There was heather, too, masses of it, but Cressida would have to wait until later in the year before she could see it in its full glory.

Piers made no attempt to get out of the car but sat staring out at the scene before him, tapping gently on the steering-wheel with his long, brown fingers. He gave a sudden, impatient sigh.

'I wish to apologise for what happened the other evening,' he said harshly, almost as though he wanted to get the words out as quickly as possible. He didn't turn his head, and his strongly marked profile was silhouetted stern and proud against a distant curtain of pine-trees. He lifted his chin a little as he went on, 'I imagine my behaviour must have offended you, and I just wanted to reassure you that nothing like it will ever happen again.'

Cressida stared at him in amazement, her heart beginning to thump disconcertingly fast. 'Offended her', had he said? How could he have got it so wrong? It wasn't his 'behaviour' as he put it, which had offended her. Quite the reverse, if only he knew.

She thought rapidly. Now he had unwittingly given

her the opportunity she had been waiting for, she must take it with both hands, whatever the consequences.

'That pub, where we had lunch . . .'

Piers turned now, his face alight with surprise at the apparent and abrupt change of subject. Cressida met his eyes directly—thank goodness he could not hear how fast her heart was beating! She put up her hand to hide the tell-tale pulse in her neck as she asked with a calmness she certainly did not feel, 'Did you take your wife there a lot? Was that how you knew it so well?'

'My *wife*?' He looked utterly stunned.

'Well—your ex-wife, then?' Cressida persevered with a burst of hope. 'Lady Aylward?'

'Lady Aylward—my *wife*?'

Piers gazed at her with an absolute astonishment which Cressida knew him well enough to know was no pretence.

'What in heaven's name do you mean—my wife? What gave you that preposterous idea?'

'That letter . . . addressed to Lady Aylward. The one I left in your study.'

Cressida's voice was faint as a welter of emotion tore through her, crimsoning her face and neck.

'I thought . . .'

The light dawned at last and Piers gave a shout of laughter.

'You thought I was married, that I had a wife hidden away somewhere—or an ex-wife no one had thought to mention to you.' He reached for her hand lying clenched in her lap, then thought better of it and withdrew his arm swiftly. He still needed reassurance.

Cressida nodded, keeping her eyes fixed, almost pleading, on his face. If only she could believe what her heart yearned to—that he hadn't and never had had a wife. But so far, he had not actually denied it.

'You haven't?' She almost held her breath as she waited for the answer she so wanted to hear.

Piers met her gaze gravely. 'I promise you, Cressida, that I never have in my whole life been married, and that I have not and never have had a wife.' He searched her face, willing her to believe him. 'Will that convince you?'

She nodded again, not daring to trust her voice.

'And the other evening?' It was his turn to seek reassurance. 'It wasn't . . .' He hesitated. 'It wasn't anything I did which made you so distant today? So unlike your normal self?'

She shook her head now, almost shyly, her green eyes wide with unspoken feelings. A long sigh escaped him and at last, gently, he reached for her hand again.

'Oh, Cressida. I was so afraid. You were so remote, almost unapproachable; I thought I'd gone too far . . . that you disliked me, even though, at the time . . .'

Cressida stared at their linked hands resting on Piers' knee.

'It wasn't only me who was distant,' she reminded him. 'You weren't exactly communicative when you came back from London. I wasn't sure what to think, and then there was the letter as well—I thought you had changed your mind about me—about us . . .'

She looked up into his face. Would he retreat again into his shell at the mere mention of his feelings? But miraculously his brow cleared, making him look almost boyish.

'And that was all that was worrying you? About my so-called wife?' He chuckled.

'Honestly.'

His hand closed more tightly round her fingers, and now she dared respond with an answering pressure. His free arm slipped gently round her shoulders and with a little sigh of release she rested her head against him. A different silence enfolded them for a while as each of them came to terms with their altered perceptions of the situation.

Suddenly Cressida twisted round in the circles of Piers' arm.

'Piers?'

His embrace strengthened. 'What?'

'Lady Aylward . . . the name on the letter. If she isn't your wife, who . . . oh, of *course*! How stupid of me! Your brother's wife . . . what was her name? Miriam?'

Piers nodded. The mere mention of his sister-in-law's name was enough to wipe all the happiness from his face, but Cressida was too wrapped up in her own thoughts to notice.

'Oh, goodness.' She covered her face with her hands in self-condemnation and relief. 'Why didn't I realise, instead of rushing to all the wrong conclusions? Lady Hugo Aylward—Miriam—not Lady Piers.'

She shook her head in disbelief and grinned up at Piers, only to start back at the blank expression on his face.

'That letter, and the phone call,' she ventured, 'were they connected in some way? Was that why you had to rush off to London and why you were so upset? She's not coming here, is she? Was that why the letter was sent to the Priory?'

Piers eased his arm from behind Cressida's shoulders and rested his chin on his hand, elbows propped stiffly on his knees.

'Yes, they were connected, and no, she's not coming back, not if I have anything to do with it.'

He stretched out his long legs and pulled a face. 'Let's go for a walk, and I'll try to explain. I owe you that, at least.'

He caught hold of her hand again as they set out along a grassy track leading in the direction of the pine woods. Cressida walked along by his side, her head in a whirl. If Piers hadn't been so preoccupied with his own concerns she felt she could have taken off, dancing along the path and singing aloud with joy as her secret heart was doing.

She kept a firm grip of his hand, reluctant to let it go. That first kiss hadn't just been like the mayfly, born in a swift moment only to die on the wing. He really did feel something for her.

'Piers?'

Her voice brought him back to earth.

'Sorry—I was miles away.' He smiled absently down at her.

'Where are we going? Anywhere in particular?'

'I thought we'd have a look at the sea—just beyond those trees. We're only a mile or two along the coast from Dunwich.'

Cressida wrinkled her brow thoughtfully.

'Isn't that the village which has been washed away over the centuries?'

Piers nodded. 'It used to be a great port in medieval times—monasteries, churches—a very prosperous place. Now there's hardly anything of it left. I'll show you one day. There's a legend that, if you listen hard at midnight, you can hear the bells of the drowned churches tolling beneath the waves.'

Cressida's imagination was caught at once. 'Have you ever heard them? Shall we try one night?'

Piers laughed. 'If you like—I don't promise anything, though. What a romantic you are!'

'Am I? I'd never given it much thought,' Cressida confessed, 'but I suppose I like a fairy-story as much as the next person.'

But what was uppermost in her mind was far from being a fairy-story.

'You did say you would explain about your sister-in-law,' she reminded Piers, determined to get to the truth of what had caused him so much anxiety.

'I did, didn't I?'

'Please don't if you'd rather not,' Cressida said quickly. 'It's none of my business—I don't want to pry.'

Piers sighed, his pace slowing down while he collected his thoughts.

'No, I'm sure you don't. As a matter of fact, I think you have been incredibly understanding in putting up with all my moods.' A wan smile appeared momentarily. 'The phone call the other evening—that was Miriam, as I told you. She wanted to come and see me at the Priory, but I didn't want her upsetting everything . . . or you.'

'I could have manged,' Cressida averred stoutly.

'I'm sure you would—or at least you would have tried. But she can be pretty disruptive when she puts her mind to it . . . no, I don't want her here,' Piers ended sharply. 'Not ever again.'

'What did she want?'

'What does she ever want? More money. As much as she can lay her hands on. She seemed to think she was owed another large helping of Hugo's non-existent estate . . . so I agreed to see her at the solicitor's offices to try to rid myself and the Priory of her unreasonable demands once and for all.'

'Did . . . did she have a case?'

Piers smiled grimly. 'We managed to beat her down. I think she got the message—and quite honestly, there's not a lot more in the kitty, not for her, not for me either.'

And that wasn't all. Miriam had also told Piers that

in her opinion she was the one who should have been given Cressida's job. She wanted to keep her clutches on the Priory by any means possible, 'And she even tried to bribe me by saying she wouldn't press for the extra money if I gave her your salary instead. She considered she was suitable for the job in every way—she had all the right contacts, for a start.'

Piers stopped and jabbed his heel into a tussock of heather. 'I know all about her contacts,' he said in a tone of disgust. 'And the further they stay from here, the better. Terrible people, her so-called friends . . .' He shuddered. 'Those days are over, thank goodness.'

'She won't make any more trouble, will she?'

'Who can tell with Miriam? Greed is what keeps her going—and if she thinks she can squeeze anything from me, nothing will stop her trying.'

And Cressida had wondered why he had come back so depressed.

'I am sorry,' she said quietly. Then she remembered something else. 'That letter—someone must have expected her to be at the Priory. There hasn't been any other mail for her since I've been here.'

'I gather she told some of her chums she was paying me a visit—no doubt that was from someone intending to invite themselves to stay . . . someone hoping it would be back to the good old days. Parties from morning to night and right through to the next morning. Oh, God, Cressida, I can't tell you what it was like.'

No wonder there's no money left, Cressida thought sadly. Still, at least she could do her small bit to put something back into what Piers had called the 'kitty'. And she was determined to pull out all the stops to bring in as many visitors as possible.

They had been walking along the edge of the pine wood, but Cressida had been concentrating so hard on what Piers had been telling her that she hadn't noticed that the trees were thinning out and they were approaching an area of sand dunes. Now, breasting the shallow incline, the North Sea was suddenly ahead of them, stretching out to the horizon, grey and smooth. The sight put all other thoughts from her mind.

'Oh, look—the sea!'

She clutched Piers' arm unthinkingly with both hands, her green eyes shining with delight.

'Good heavens, Cressida,' Piers laughed. 'Anyone would think you'd never seen it before. I thought you came from Kent—that's almost surrounded by sea, unless my memory's playing me tricks.'

'Yes, I know.' She pulled him along impatiently. 'But you know what it's like when you live in a place—you hardly ever go on trips. I don't know when I last stood on a beach. Come on, let's go and paddle!' She pulled at his arm, but he did not make any move to follow. Instead, his grip tightened on her arm as he pulled her round to face him, raising her chin so that he could look deep into her wide, wondering eyes.

'Oh, Cressida!'

His lips came down on hers then, and this time there was no uncertainty between them. She knew, exultantly, that she could—would—respond to him without restraint or doubt.

A little way ahead there was a secluded depression in the dunes protected by an outcrop of gorse, and, his lips still brushing her face and her blowing hair, he led her towards it. In a kind of golden daze Cressida allowed herself to be guided to the sheltered hollow, every nerve acutely alive to the sensations aroused in her by the strong arm round her waist, the warm lips against her skin.

Piers dropped on to one knee, holding out his hand in wordless invitation, and she sank to the ground beside him, her fingers clutching at his in a tense, tremulous movement.

She lay on her back, looking up at him in wonder, and Piers propped himself on one elbow by her side to stroke back the thick, dark hair from her forehead, his mouth curving into a slow smile. Their eyes met, and she was lost, drowned like the submerged churches of Dunwich in the sea-grey depths where glints of gold mirrored the lights struck by the sun on the restless waves beyond the shore.

She let her hand curve round the back of his neck, moving her fingers sensuously to trace the fine lines beside his eyes and delighting in the feel of the smooth brown skin under her touch.

Her eyes dwelt hungrily on the strongly moulded contours of his face and the dark brows under the straight-falling fair hair which she pushed back impatiently as it fell over his eyes. And all the while Piers made no movement, but seemed content to drink in every line of her face as though he had never really seen it before and needed to imprint it on to his memory.

Then, as she lightly caressed his mouth, he could restrain himself no longer. He seized her hand and began kissing each fingertip in turn before pressing his lips to the palm of her hand, the softness of her inner arm, the pulse beating frenziedly at the base of her neck.

'Oh, Piers!'

She moved convulsively against him and only then did his lips come down at last to meet her own, hesitating just once as though he were still unsure of himself—of her—but her yearning mouth left him in no doubt and with a little laugh of delight he crushed it with his, the barriers down at last, Cressida thought in triumph as her hand strayed over his shoulder and down the taut muscles of his back.

The whole world seemed to melt away at his kiss—the

distant sound of the waves breaking on the stony beach beyond the dunes, the occasional cry of a gull, the murmur of bees in the gorse . . . all faded away, leaving just the two of them locked in a timeless embrace beneath a whirling, blazing sun.

She pressed her swelling breasts against his hard body and gasped as she felt his burning lips trace the path of his fingers as they slowly undid the buttons of her thin shirt, arousing deep in her body a fierce, burning pain. The sun beat down on her bare skin, on the silvery lights in the fair head cradled on her shoulder, and an ecstatic joy swept over her, so powerful her whole body trembled.

Piers raised his head, looking questioningly into her eyes, but not moving the hand lightly but so possessively covering her aching breast.

'You don't mind?'

For answer Cressida rested her own hand on his, moving her head slowly from side to side, unable to speak from pure joy.

'You're so beautiful . . . I never thought . . .'

A deep sigh escaped him, then he added, so softly she could scarcely hear him "There's language in her eye, her cheek, her lip . . ." dropping a lingering kiss on each feature as he named it.

'Poetry?' Cressida murmured—nothing he did would surprise her any more.

'Shakespeare . . . "Nay,"' he went on, ' "her foot speaks; her wanton spirits look out at every joint and motive of her body." '

His hand, caressing and exploring, travelled the length of her body and she heard a groan of sensual delight—hers, she realised with a start—as she arched her back to his touch. Bright stars and whorls exploded behind her eyelids, closed to withstand the onslaught on her senses, every nerve strung to concert pitch by the stroking, searching movement of his fingers.

How long they lay there, Cressida couldn't have told. Time ceased to have any meaning as he held her against him in this endless, passionate embrace, close enough for her to feel the pounding of his heart as though within her own breast. And she knew, now, that he wanted her urgently and also that he was holding back—the time for total surrender was not yet. It was enough to lie together within the sound of the far-breaking waves and know that when that moment came . . .

Her thoughts went no further than her immediate and exultant response to the man holding her in his arms—the man whom she had until today, this magical, unbelievable day, decided was so aloof, detached, cold . . .

A laugh bubbled to her lips and was quickly silenced by Piers' warm mouth on hers.

'Oh, Piers,' she breathed, winding her arms even more tightly round the spare, hard body lying by her side. 'I'm so happy . . . so marvellously happy.' She moved her hands to hold his face between them and gazed deep into his eyes, as though drinking her fill from the sea-grey, glinting depths.

'So why laugh?' Piers scolded her with mock severity. 'I don't think this . . .' he bent to her lips once more, 'Or this . . . ' and dropped a kiss on the soft breast beneath his hand, 'are any laughing matter.'

Cressida moved her head lazily to deny this accusation. 'I wasn't laughing at you—or us . . . it was something I remembered.'

'Something you can share?'

Gradually they were coming back to earth, but united now in a bond so sweet that Cressida could have no regrets. There would be other even sweeter moments to cherish, but for now she was content simply to relish the transformation in this strange, fascinating man.

'I was just thinking . . .' she reached up and kissed him again to convince herself she had not dreamt the whole thing ' . . . that until this afternoon—with the possible exception of a few moments one particular evening—I'd always thought of you as cold . . . aloof, taciturn, remote.'

Piers gazed at her in alarm.

'You make me sound like a dictionary definition of something rather unpleasant.'

'You hadn't ever given me much encouragement to think of you in a less forbidding way—even you must admit that.'

Piers grimaced. 'I suppose not.' He sighed. 'I haven't had a lot of practice in the art of dalliance.'

Cressida giggled. 'Dalliance? Is that what it was? How very Shakespearean, like those lines you quoted just now. *Troilus and Cressida*, I suppose?'

Piers nodded. 'Not an entirely admirable character, I'm afraid, your namesake, but she had quite an effect on the poor, gullible menfolk.' He paused, then added teasingly, 'There's another line I like, too.'

'Tell me.'

He caught her hand and held it to his lips, shaking his head solemnly.

'No, I think I'll keep it for another time.'

Another time! Cressida's heart lurched at the words. Oh, yes, let there be another time, and another . . . on and on . . .

A light breeze from the sea ruffled her hair, and she struggled into a sitting position, her shirt still open, luxuriating in the cooling air on her hot skin still burning from his kisses.

Piers' eyes wandered appraisingly over her body.

' "Wanton" was the word the Bard used,' he said casually, 'and I know what he meant.'

Cressida pouted in mock offence. 'Sorry, sir.'

She began doing up the buttons, kneeling up to tuck the shirt into her skirt-top, but not before, with an almost feline swiftness, Piers moved behind her, twining his arms round her again, kissing the nape of her neck beneath the tumbled hair . . . moving his hands upwards from her waist . . .

With a quick intake of breath Cressida leant sensuously against him for an instant, before twisting away and scrambling to her feet. All at once she felt she needed a moment or two to herself, not so much to regain her composure as to savour the enchantment—to imprint it on her soul before it slipped from her grasp for ever. She climbed to the top of the dunes and gazed out to the distant horizon, the restless sea the colour of his eyes now breaking in white horses in the freshening breeze. She wrapped her arms round her body and Piers, watching her, restrained his instinctive desire to join her, content to drink in every line of her body silhouetted against the sky.

She felt his eyes on her and turned to face him, and then, hand-fast and wordlessly, they started to walk slowly back.

CHAPTER EIGHT

THE rest of that day passed in a sort of daze. Cressida was profoundly thankful she did not have to meet anybody, even—perhaps especially—Mary, who wasn't due back till the following morning, as the telltale glow would have been a clear beacon signalling her ecstasy to the whole world.

How was she going to concentrate on her work again? She had made no attempt to do anything on their return to the Priory, but had spent the rest of the afternoon curled up in one of the big leather armchairs in Piers' study, reading one of his books as he attended to some urgent business.

They had cooked supper together, shared a bottle of wine from the cellar and sat talking quietly, touching one another from time to time, but sensing this was not the moment to give rein to the passions each knew were simmering just below the surface of their outward calm.

As the evening drew on, Cressida's heart began to beat faster. What would happen later? She wasn't even sure what she wanted to happen, whether she was ready for a night of love so soon after the magic of the afternoon which had left such precious memories she wanted to keep unblurred.

'I . . . I think I'll go and get some sleep, now,' she faltered when her eyes could hardly keep open from exhaustion after all the emotions of the day. Piers met her gaze full on and pulled her to her feet and into his arms.

'All my instincts are crying out to take you with me,' he said softly, burying his face in her hair, 'but that would be selfish.'

He held her away from, him and ran his hands down her arms, making her shiver with delight. 'There's no hurry, though, is there? We'll both be here in the morning.'

So he did feel as she did! Cressida's heart leapt at the discovery, then she sighed. 'So will Mary Bryant.'

Piers grinned. 'We'll just have to put on a good act—the arrogant baronet and his docile assistant . . . just like before.' He ducked as Cressida took a swing at him, her eyes flashing green sparks.

'Me, docile? I thought I was supposed to be wanton, or had you forgotten already?'

A peal of joyous laughter rang out as Piers crushed her to his chest again, covering her face with kisses.

'How could I forget—oh, my love . . .'

For a long minute they stood locked in a fierce embrace as an unspoken longing hung in the air between them. Then, almost abruptly, he dropped his arms to his sides.

'Go and catch up on your sleep, or I won't be answerable for what might happen.'

The temptation to stay with him almost overcame her, but with a mighty effort of will Cressida tore herself away, pausing just once in the doorway to look back at the tall figure, imprinting on her very soul the burning grey eyes beneath the dark brows, the mouth which only moments before had been pressed so ardently to hers . . . then, with a gasp, she fled back to her own room and a dream-haunted sleep.

Mercifully Piers was nowhere to be seen the following morning, and Cressida had regained enough of her customary composure to face Mary and her questions in what she hoped appeared her normal manner.

'Well, how did it go?'

Mary had scarcely got inside the kitchen before the eager interrogation began.

'Fine,' Cressida replied brightly. 'He seemed to enjoy my cooking, and we had a very pleasant evening.'

Truth to tell, so much had happened since the evening of the supper—Thursday, had it been, or Friday?—that she could hardly recall the details Mary was so anxious to hear.

'What do you mean, a "pleasant evening"?' Mary demanded. 'That doesn't tell me a thing.' She reached for her apron and tied it firmly round her waist, fixing her keen eyes on Cressida's face. 'Did Sir Piers unbend at all? Or was he his usual upright and proper self?'

Cressida smiled reminiscently and felt mean at having to fob Mary off, but she couldn't tell her, not yet, however good a friend she was. Her mind was still in a ferment—a delicious, secret turmoil that didn't want to share its memories with anyone. But some time, maybe later today, Mary would be sure to see the two of them together, and there was no way they could completely disguise the change in their relationship. She would have to say something.

'He was a bit taken aback at first,' Cressida told Mary, 'and for a moment I did think he might turn tail and run. I had the kitchen all smartened up with flowers and candles—it did really look very pretty.'

'But he didn't did he?'

'He didn't. We actually got on very well after our usual sticky start. He talked a lot, for him, and I think we both felt we'd got to know one another a lot better. It should make things easier in the future, anyway. At least, I hope so.'

How prosaic it sounded; almost too prosaic to be

convincing. Cressida turned away and busied herself putting things away in a drawer the other side of the kitchen to disguise any telltale hint on her face of the true state of their new-found relationship, and if Mary had any suspicions, she kept them to herself.

And, in any case, what *was* the state of their relationship? Knowing Piers, some little thing would be enough to make him pull up the drawbridge again. Casual relationships just weren't in his nature, she was sure, and why should she think that what happened between them yesterday was a sign of anything deeper?

I must keep busy, she told herself firmly, once she had made her escape from under Mary's eagle eye. She longed to see Piers . . . was he regretting the episode altogether by now? Was that why he was keeping out of her way, so as not to have to tell her it had all been a mistake? He's over there somewhere, she kept telling herself—she had seen the Land Rover and the car still in the garage.

It could, though, be from tact or simply prudence that he was keeping his distance. He didn't *know* how she was feeling. If only she could tell him . . .

Cressida's fingers slowed to a halt over the typewriter keyboard and her eyes stared unseeing through the office window, coming to rest on the soothing green of the distant trees. It almost seemed like a dream now. She heard again the sound of waves breaking on the shore beyond the dunes, smelt the scent of gorse and bracken, and then . . .

She wrapped her arms round her body in a desperate attempt to recapture a glimmer of that fire his embrace had kindled deep within her, and a yearning welled up to feel his lips pressing on hers again. Something in the depths of her stirred even at the memory—where was he, and why wouldn't he come and see her?

She leapt up, unable to keep still any longer, and went over to the window, peering out in the hope of catching at least a glimpse of the tall figure who haunted her thoughts, but there was no sign of him, and eventually, with a deep sigh, she returned to her desk.

It wasn't until the evening that Piers came to seek Cressida out as she was in the kitchen making a risotto for their supper.

'What have you been doing all day?'

The strong arm slipped round her waist as she was stirring the pan on the stove, and he kissed the nape of her neck. That was all she needed to know, and she leant against him with a little sigh of contentment.

'Don't distract me,' she teased, 'or I'll burn the risotto.'

'Blow the risotto.'

Impatiently Piers pushed the pan aside and seized the spoon from Cressida's grasp, imprisoning her fingers in his as he pulled her close.

Cressida lifted her face, trembling slightly at the nearness of him.

'It's been a long day,' he murmured as his lips met hers, brushing them gently as though renewing their acquaintance. Cressida reached up and wound her arm round his neck in an ardent response of her own to his tender embrace.

'It's no good,' she said at last, disentangling herself from his encircling arms.

'I think it's very good,' Piers retorted as he made a grab for her hand. 'Come here . . .'

'No, Piers—let me go for a minute. I've still got things to do—unless you're going to have supper by yourself again. In any case . . .' she flounced away from his clutches ' . . . I thought the way to a man's heart was through his stomach—or so my mother taught me.'

'Very practical lady, your mother,' Piers conceded, 'but she should have told you there were other ways too. You must remind me to show you some time.' He prowled restlessly round the room, waiting for Cressida to stop attending to the pans.

'That will be very nice,' Cressida said primly, 'but for now, I suggest you sit down and have a glass of wine. You're making me nervous, wandering about like that.'

'You're so sensible,' Piers sighed, leaning back in his chair and watching her drain the rice before mixing it into the other ingredients. 'Have you no romance in your soul?'

'Plenty,' she returned. 'In fact, only yesterday you were scolding me for having too much when we were talking about Dunwich—if you remember?'

'Yesterday . . . as though I could forget.' Piers spoke softly, content for the moment to let his eyes rest on her as she put the final touches to their meal. 'But catering isn't what I asked you here to do—we should have gone out somewhere.'

'Maybe in a day or two—thanks, that would be lovely, but with the opening day fixed now, there's still a lot to do . . . unless you'll change your mind,' she added diffidently, with a doubtful glance in his direction, 'and consider . . .'

'No, Cressida, I'm sorry, but I made my mind up long ago about that. What happened yesterday makes no difference to my decision as far as the Priory's concerned.'

'Oh, well.' She shrugged helplesly and stared at him for a moment, terrified the old reticence would return and he would shut her out again. But he just smiled a trifle wryly in tacit admission of his own unreasonableness, then changed the subject in the infuriating way he had when confronted with something disagreeable.

The rest of the evening passed happily enough, but the magic of the day had gone into cold storage for the time being and Cressida cursed her thoughtless tongue for making the suggestion that he might be prepared to take a more active role now, and help her with the visitors. She might have known he'd be too stubborn to change his mind on that.

Piers, too, seemed to be preoccupied with something, and it wasn't till they were having coffee in the study that she got a hint of what it was.

It was her turn to watch him from her seat in the big chair she always chose, as he methodically prepared and poured the coffee. What a complicated man he was with his abrupt changes of mood—but at least he had allowed her across the drawbridge now, to stand just within the marble walls which protected the privacy of his inermost heart.

She smiled up at him as he handed her her cup.

'Thanks—it's a great treat, this. Your coffee always tastes much better than mine.'

Piers acknowledged the compliment with a brief smile, then frowned. He made as though to sit on the arm of Cressida's chair, then thought better of it and went over to his old place by the window, staring out with his hands clasped behind his back.

Not again! Cressida couldn't bear it, and this time she wasn't going to let him shut her out, not if she could prevent it. She put her cup down and went quietly over to join him, putting her hand on his shoulder.

'Piers, what is it? Have I said something? Do you . . .' she faltered, 'do you regret what happened yesterday? Does it make things difficult for you—I'll try to forget if you think we should . . .?'

'Oh, no—don't think that.'

Horrified by the very idea, Piers enfolded her in his

arms and she rested her cheek against his broad chest for a moment before looking up into his worried face. The grey eyes were distant—no golden sparks to light them today.

'You're so good for me, Cressida. It's only too easy to shut myself away . . . and of course I've no regrets about yesterday. How could I?'

He caught her by the shoulders and traced the line of her cheekbone with one gentle finger.

'Why are you worried?' she asked softly. 'I know you are, so there's no use trying to hide it. Is it Lady Aylward again—is she making more demands?'

Piers shook his head. 'No, not this time.' His features lightened with an unexpected grin. 'About the first time it hasn't been anything to do with her.'

'Then what . . .?'

'Some problems have arisen over my latest book—nothing drastic, really. I've just got used to brooding when there's something on my mind. No one has ever offered to share my problems before.'

Cressida smoothed the lines on his forehead with a caress of her hand.

'Nothing I can help with—typing or anything?'

Piers smiled at her gratefully.

'That's a very kind offer, considering the amount you have to do already and with no help from me. But it's not that kind of problem. It's something I'll have to sort out with my publishers. Tomorrow, I think . . . I'll have to go to London again.'

'Oh—so soon?'

The words slipped out unthinkingly. She had only just found him, the real Piers, and he was disappearing again already. His arms tightened round her and he gave a light laugh of pure happiness.

'Dearest Cressida—no one has ever missed me

before. It's a new experience, and I can't begin to explain what it feels like.' He kissed her tenderly. 'I'll be back, though, as soon as I can. Probably the day after tomorrow. I'll let you know if it takes any longer.'

They stood side by side, arms round one another, gazing out at the garden, a peaceful haven in the fading light. Piers cupped her face in his hand and dropped a caress on her eyelids.

'Coffee's going cold,' Cressida murmured, leaning against him. 'Seems a pity . . .'

'I told you you had no romance in your soul.'

'Waste not, want not,' she retorted pertly. 'You employed me to save money, Sir Piers.'

She heard the sharp intake of breath as his arm dropped. Had she gone too far? Her tongue had run away with her again, taking liberties with a subject far too delicate to treat with such flippancy. She should have known that.

'I apologise,' she said quickly, with an anxious look at the stern face. 'I didn't mean to joke about it—it was thoughtless of me.' She almost held her breath as she waited for his response. It took so little to make him retreat inside his protective armour, and, whatever her feelings for him, he was her employer, she must never forget, a proud man whose ancient ancestry lent him an assurance and authority she must respect even in these days of so-called equality. That apart, he hadn't been brought up in the teasing informality of ordinary, happy family life. She must not treat him as she would one of her own contemporaries.

His hand slipped under her chin, raising her face implacably to meet his. His eyes were expressionless stones and she felt her legs shake—she had made him angry, and with such a thoughtless little phrase, too. She could have bitten her tongue out.

'Don't joke about money again, please, Cressida,' he said in a flat tone. 'It's the sort of remark my sister-in-law would make, and I don't find the subject a cause for amusement.'

He moved away to pick up his cup, draining it at a single gulp. 'You're right—it's cold,' he remarked in distaste.

And that wasn't all that was chilled, Cressida thought dismally, watching him collect up the papers he would need for his meeting with his publisher. It took so little to extinguish the faint embers of warmth she had been able to kindle in his marble heart. Would she have to begin all over again?

This evening, anyway, the fire was out. She drank her own tepid coffee and put down her cup.

'I hope it all goes well tomorrow,' she told him quietly. 'And I didn't mean . . .' She spread her hands in a helpless gesture.

Piers raised his eyes from the papers on his desk to meet hers briefly.

'I know——' He smiled ruefully, but without warmth. 'I guess I'm just a little sensitive on that particular matter. You'll have to forgive me for being touchy.'

He made no attempt to approach her, or kiss her goodbye, and although longing to cross the divide between them, to reach out and touch him, Cressida held back. Please God there would be other opportunities to heal this breach and regain his trust, and at least she knew that the drawbridge could be crossed, given the right strategy and endless patience.

Piers left early the following morning. Cressida knew he probably would, but even so she couldn't repress a feeling of disappointment when she saw the empty study and vacant space in the garage where the Land Rover usually stood. Still, some time to herself would give her the chance to gather her thoughts together and prepare herself for his return and whatever mood she might find him in.

She had worked so hard the day before that there wasn't a great deal of correspondence to catch up on, and by thc afternoon there was nothing left to do except a backlog of filing, a job she hated and always left until the last possible moment. No chance of her desk being as orderly as Piers', she thought regretfully as she tidied up the sheaves of letters, invoices and odd bits of paper that seemed to find their way on to every spare inch of space. Still, everyone had their own way of working, and at least she wasn't behind with her arrangements. In fact, everything was so far—she mentally crossed her fingers—going according to plan.

Cressida glanced up at the big calendar she had pinned up on the wall, and her stomach lurched at the sight of the fat red ring round a date only . . . what was it? She counted carefully, even though she knew only too well how long there was to go: three weeks to the Grand Opening. July the fifteenth. Red Letter Day.

She had sent the announcement, with publicity material, to every possible interested organisation, periodical, radio station and television company, and if nobody came after that, God forbid, it could hardly be her fault.

If only Piers would co-operate, do a bit of publicising of his own, or at least agree to be present at the start, for moral support if for no other reason. Always her thoughts returned to him . . .

What was that? Cressida paused, file in either hand, and listened intently. Surely it was the sound of a car engine? No one was expected. Had Piers come back already? Scarcely anyone else ever drove right up to the main door—all the locals went round to the back.

She put down the papers and almost ran out into the passage outside her office to peer through the window which gave on to the courtyard . . . and stopped.

That wasn't the Land Rover, but a spanking new little white car, very racy, very expensive, which was just skidding to a halt outside. Whoever could it be? Surely none of Piers' acquaintances drove anything like that—*he* hadn't gone quite mad, surely, and bought it for himself?

Cressida watched, fascinated, as the driver's door opened and out stepped one of the most elegant figures she had ever seen outside the pages of *Vogue*. Every inch of her visitor, from the deliberately disarranged coiffure to the tips of her high-heeled sandals, positively shouted extravgance and style.

She was wearing a beautifully cut jumpsuit of what appeared to be the softest suede, and was trailing a long silk scarf knotted casually round her neck. She walked up to the house with an easy familiarity, not looking round as a stranger would have done. This woman had been here before. The sun struck sparks from the heavy gold bangle on the thin wrist raised to the bell.

Reluctantly Cressida made her way round to the Hall—the imperious ringing would have to be answered. She glanced down in dismay at her own outfit, for, knowing she would be on her own all day, she had on her oldest jeans with a faded shirt which really should have been thrown out long ago—too tatty even for a jumble sale. What a shabby picture she presented by contrast.

Cressida felt a certain relief that she had at least had this preview of the visitor who was now waiting for admittance with increasing impatience if the insistent ringing were anything to go by.

Whoever could it be? No one Cressida had ever had anything to do with in connection with her work, unless one of the glossy magazines had sent someone up to do a recce—but surely they would have made an appointment first?

Cressida struggled with the bolt and locks. She hardly ever used this door—it was so much easier to go in and out by the back way—and pulled it open just as the woman's hand was poised to ring again.

'At last.'

Cressida found herself looking into the face of a woman some years older than herself, though the clever and painstaking use of make-up was clearly designed to disguise the fact.

Her hair was dark chestnut with auburn highlights where the sun caught it, and her eyes under the beautifully shaped eyebrows and soft green eyeshadow were brown, but not soft and gentle as so many brown eyes could be, but hard and appraising as a man's.

Light lines of discontent rather than humour were visible beneath the careful *maquillage* round the eyes, and there was a hint of petulance about the red mouth. It was a brittle, hard face, not one which called up any answering warmth, and Cressida felt immediately on her guard before they had even exchanged a word.

I'm sorry to have kept you waiting. Instinctively the polite words formed themselves on her lips, but she bit them back. Something about the almost imperceptible narrowing of the visitor's eyes as she took in Cressida's dishevelled appearance raised her mental hackles. Instead, she drew herself up to her full height, overtopping her visitor by several inches.

'Can I help you?'

Her apparent self-assurance seemed to disconcert the other woman who, frowning, took a couple of steps backwards. Cressida followed up her advantage by standing quite still and waiting silently for her reply.

Long, red-tipped fingers adjusted the scarf round her neck.

'I've come to see Sir Piers Aylward.' The voice was husky, and she spoke slowly, as though using an instrument long practised in attracting men, Cressida thought nastily, having taken an instant dislike to the speaker. She smiled sweetly.

'I'm afraid he's away at present, and I'm not expecting him back today.'

'*You're* not . . .' The emphasis implied a definite contempt. Who are you, were the unuttered words, to express opinions about the movements of Sir Piers Aylward?

'I think I'd better introduce myself,' Cressida went on pleasantly, making the most of her chance to take the upper hand. 'I'm Cressida Heaton—I work for Sir Piers. I'm in charge of his scheme for opening the Priory to visitors. Is it something to do with that about which you wish to see him? If so, I'm sure I can tell you anything you wish to know.'

The cool eyes widened slightly, one eyebrow raised.

'I see . . .' The woman frowned. 'It really is most inconvenient.' She tapped a fingernail impatiently against her teeth and considered the situation in silence for some moments. Then she flashed Cressida a brilliant smile.

'What a good thing I brought my overnight bag. You just get on with whatever it is you have to do, Miss . . . Miss Heaton?'

Cressida nodded, her breath taken away by the blatant presumption. Who was this person to take such liberties?

'I'll go and make myself comfy in the spare room. No

need to show me the way.'

She turned and tripped back to her car, perfuming the air with wafts of expensive scent. Over her shoulder she added, almost as an afterthought, 'Oh, in case you hadn't guessed, I'm Miriam Aylward, Lady Miriam Aylward . . . Sir Hugo's widow. No doubt Sir Piers will have told you all about me?'

She laughed gaily as she brought out a smart little case, striped with the distinctive Gucci colours—she must have been planning all along to stay the night, Cressida decided. No one brings an overnight bag on spec. if they're just calling on someone. What did she want with Piers? He had been under the distinct impression he had seen the last of her. Let's hope I can get rid of her before he comes back, was Cressida's fervent wish as she stood her ground by the front door.

'You don't want proof of my identity, do you?' Lady Aylward laughed, raising that infuriating eyebrow once again. She made as though to open her handbag.

Cressida flushed. 'No, of course not.' She hovered, uncertainly, between the other woman and the door. It wasn't really possible to prevent her entering, however loudly her instincts were warning against it.

'I suppose it's all right . . .'

'Of course, it is.' Lady Aylward's voice dropped, reassuring, persuasive. 'I'm not likely to run off with the family silver . . .' She gave a tinkly little laugh. 'Not that there's a lot left to run off with now, I don't imagine.'

A slow anger began to simmer inside Cressida, and she began to feel something of what Piers was going through. How dared she . . .? They turned to face each other on the threshold.

'Don't worry about me, Miss Heaton. I'll make my own way upstairs. I know where the sheets will be—

unless you've taken over the domestic arrangements as well.'

Cressida drew in her breath sharply at the implication in the suggestion, but Lady Aylward disappeared into the comparative gloom of the Great Hall, effectively forestalling any effective reply, and Cressida could hear the stiletto heels clacking daintily up the oak stairs to the landing above.

What was she to do now? Piers would be absolutely furious when he discovered whom she had let into the house—and not only let in, but allowed to stay. How could she get rid of this most unwelcome visitor, and what was it she wanted?

Cressida walked slowly out into the garden, knowing she wouldn't be able to settle to anything while that woman was here. She knew also why Piers found her so disturbing. Miriam Aylward was one of those people who couldn't leave anything alone. If she found Cressida in her office she would start poking about and trying to interfere in her arrangements. She mustn't forget that Miriam had already set her sights on the job itself, and although Piers had told her there was no chance of taking over, she might well try more devious means to get what she wanted.

If only Piers hadn't gone away, and if only Cressida had been able to repair the damage to their fragile relationship before he had gone off. She stared miserably at the Elizabethan garden which bore all the hallmarks of his meticulous care and artistic imagination. His coming back to find his sister-in-law in residence would hardly improve matters between the two of them, and she was quite sure that Hugo's widow would not leave until she had managed to see Piers. Why had everything got into such a muddle just now . . .?

Cressida gazed at the intricate pattern of lavender and box hedges, trying to counjure up Piers' familiar presence among the bright flowers. That enchanted afternoon by the sea seemed an eternity away already. Would she ever feel his arms round her again, or had the arrival of Miriam Aylward jeopardised all their future happiness? Deep within her Cressida knew her very presence was a threat.

Something Piers had said came back to her: 'She can be pretty disruptive when she puts her mind to it.'

Well, Cressida was on her guard now, and she would have to make sure that Lady Aylward would have her work cut out to disrupt her and her plans to help save the Priory from the ravages already brought about by Miriam and her husband.

CHAPTER NINE

EXOTIC smells tantalised Cressida's nostrils as she made her way to the kitchen later that day to get herself something to eat. She had deliberately left Lady Aylward to make her own arrangements, and she certainly appeared to have done just that.

'Ah, there you are, Miss Heaton.' Miriam Aylward spotted her the moment she appeared in the doorway. 'Tell me, where do you keep the garlic? I can't find it anywhere.'

She had obviously had a pretty good search, though. Cressida was brought up short by the amazing sight that met her eyes as she came into the room. Miriam Aylward seemed to have used every single pan and basin, and ransacked all the cupboards in her culinary efforts.

'Heavens!' Cressida burst out involuntarily. 'What a lot of *things*!'

Miriam let out a merry laugh and peered at something in a bowl which she tasted with one delicate finger.

'Mmmm . . .' She looked up at Cressida from under her long, mascaraed eyelashes. 'Garlic, darling?'

'Oh . . . yes.'

Cressida found it in the pantry and put in on the table.

'That looks delicious,' she conceded, trying not to sound grudging.

'Won't be long now.' Piers' sister-in-law bustled about, crushing the garlic which she added to some other concoction already simmering on the stove. She looked across at Cressida.

'You don't mind, do you? I don't know what you were going to have, but I suddenly felt really hungry . . . and I do like pottering about in other people's kitchens.'

'You mean you want me to share it with you?' Cressida asked bluntly.

'There's far too much for one—I never was one to know when to stop.' Miriam Aylward laughed. 'It seems silly us cooking separate meals, don't you think?'

She'd won again, Cressida thought in some disgust as she laid the table—for two. Did she always get her own way in everything?

'So tell me,' Miriam asked her when they had almost finished the meal, which had been just as delicious as it had smelt, 'how are you getting on with my stuffy old brother-in-law? You must tell me what it is you actually do here—and I'd be most interested to know what plans you've made to lure hapless tourists to this ancient monument. Going to save the family fortunes, are you?'

I must be careful, Cressida thought, and not give anything away. She decided to ignore the first of the other woman's questions. Her relationship with Piers was none of her business. Nor was any of it, come to that, and she mustn't forget that Miriam Aylward had had her eye on the job of administrator and even now maybe hadn't given up all hopes of dislodging Cressida. There was obviously no way she was going to be dissuaded from trying to find out as much as possible . . . so, it would be better to tell her what she, Cressida, wanted her to know rather than let her come to all the wrong conclusions.

'I don't know about saving the family fortunes.' Cressida met the brown eyes levelly. 'But Sir Piers has employed *me*——' here she gave the word a slight emphasis, just to let her inquisitor know exactly where she stood '—to work out a scheme to get people to come and visit the Priory. And that's all there is to it so far. If we can make a success of it, we might branch out further—provide teas, have a craft shop, a garden centre . . . I don't know yet. We'll have to see.'

Miriam Aylward raised her eyebrows and rolled a crumb with her scarlet-tipped finger.

'I notice you say "we". I can't believe Piers is actually involved in all this, too? Not his style at all.'

She smiled as though at some private memories, and an unexpected pang of jealousy stabbed Cressida at the realisation that she'd had no part in Piers' life before this summer. Other people, even Miriam, knew his ways and idiosyncrasies better than she did.

'Sir Piers has left me in charge,' she returned stiffly. 'His time is taken up with writing . . . and the garden.'

'The garden?' This was news to Miriam. 'This I must see before I go.' Again that brittle laugh. 'Not like his brother, is he? Not in the least.' She paused, pursing her lips. 'Funny, isn't it, how two brothers can be so totally different? And I mean totally.'

'Never having met Sir Hugo,' Cressida said, 'I wouldn't know.'

'I'm sure you've been told enough, though.' The brown eyes lost their sparkle as they gazed at some sad, inward memory, and for the first time Cressida saw her not as the archvillainess everyone had painted, but a woman whose marriage and highly enjoyable life-style had come to a sudden and tragic end. Whatever the rights and wrongs of the outcome of Hugo's feck-lessness, his widow was a human being with griefs and anxieties of her own. She bit her lip as she smiled wryly at Cressida.

'Don't worry about me—just a passing shadow. We used to have such times here . . .' She darted a sharp look at Cressida. 'I don't suppose it's exactly a bundle of laughs now—no . . .' she raised a hand, seeing Cressida about to leap to Piers' defence, 'I won't make you say anything disloyal—but I'm not that dim, dear. I know how things must be.'

I hope she doesn't, Cressida thought in alarm, or is she just fishing? She managed to get Miriam to change the subject by a non-committal reply, but Piers' sister-in-law was not to be put off so easily.

They were having coffee in what was known as the 'Boudoir', a small, elegant drawing-room already prepared for the visitors' tour, when Miriam turned to Cressida with a mischievous expression.

'I don't suppose you've had a lot of fun while you've been here, have you?'

'Fun? I don't know . . .' Cressida was puzzled. 'I'm not here to have fun, am I? Just to get on with my job.'

'Good heavens, girl! You sound as if "fun" were something wicked.' Miriam peered worriedly at her. 'You're not some religious freak, are you? You don't consider music and dancing works of the devil—sins, that sort of thing?'

'Good lord, no.' Cressida laughed. 'No—what I meant was, I'm here to do a job, not indulge in wild parties like—oh, I'm sorry!' She flushed and her hand flew to her mouth in dismay.

Miriam brushed her apologies aside.

'I know—wild parties like Hugo and I used to have, you were going to say. I know only too well what people will have been telling you, but it doesn't worry me, not any more. No, I had something quite different in mind.' She put her cup down impatiently on the walnut card-table at her elbow and leant forward to fix Cressida with her keen gaze. Cressida was mesmerised by the nervous movements of the narrow fingers—that was an amazing ruby on her right hand. It must have cost a fortune . . . one of Piers' pictures, for example? She forced her attention back to what Miriam was saying.

'I don't know what publicity you've organised to launch your scheme?'

Cressida opened her mouth, but Miriam waved the words aside.

'I'll be willing to bet whatever you have arranged you're not going to have a party, though—a great, splashy colourful party with lots of fun people, music, champagne . . . a ball, even . . . why not?' Miriam's eyes sparkled as the idea took hold in her mind. 'I can see it all—the Priory and Piers' precious gardens full of people all laughing and enjoying themselves, including you . . . and Piers.'

She dissolved into a peal of laughter, meeting Cressida's glum face.

'I don't think Sir Piers . . .'

'Don't tell me old Piers has infected you with his special brand of Puritan misery? Come on, Cressida, you're only young once—and Piers never was. Let yourself go. If Piers doesn't like it he can do the other thing. Retire to London, or go off on his travels until it's all over.'

'He's not intending to be here for the opening,' Cressida confessed unwillingly. 'He said he couldn't stand the thought of the Priory being trampled all over by hordes of visitors.'

Miriam nodded. 'It figures—so, there we are then. No problem. A party we shall have, with or without his blessing.'

I must stop this, Cressida thought in alarm. She

mustn't let Miriam get away with this mad idea and jeopardise all her carefully laid plans to keep the opening low-key and dignified. Only that way could she hope to win Piers' co-operation.

'We can't afford it,' she told the other woman frankly. 'I've budgeted very carefully, and there just isn't anything left . . . also, time's running out. And I've never organised a party on the scale you're suggesting.'

Surely that would be enough to put her off.

'Ah, but I have.' Miriam grinned gleefully. 'As for money, we charge exorbitant sums for coming, and with any luck we'll end up with a profit.

'We . . .' Cressida murmured faintly, furious with herself for playing right into Miriam's hands and offering her the organisation on a plate.

'Of course. You won't have to worry about a thing. Leave everything to me, my love. I may not be good at many things, but I count myself a positive expert on parties. Oh, I *am* glad I came when I did!'

She leapt out of her chair and began to dart about the room, picking things up and rearranging them until Cressida began to feel quite dizzy just watching her.

What was Piers going to say when he got back? There was no way she could hide what was in the wind, and a party organised by Miriam of all people would be enough to make him throw her out. She cast her mind back to her first day when her suggestion of a fancy dress ball had met with such instant and adamant opposition.

'Don't look so worried.' Miriam's voice brought her quickly back to the present.

She decided to make one last try to stem the flood of Miriam's enthusiasm. 'I'm not exactly worried,' she said, standing up to take advantage of her height—the only advantage she felt she possessed over the other woman. 'But I don't think it is such a good idea. It's kind of you to take an interest, but . . .'

'Good God, Miriam! What the hell are you doing here?'

Both women swung round, Cressida's heart in her mouth.

'Piers!' they cried simultaneously, and Cressida was too shocked to see the glint in Miriam's eyes as she registered Cressida's use of his Christian name. She missed nothing, filing away such information as this in her mind for future reference and possible use. Meanwhile, her amused gaze rested on Piers, who stood in the doorway looking from one to the other in disbelief.

Cressida's overwhelming desire was to rush up to him and throw herself into his arms. They had parted so coolly, and she needed more than anything the reassurance that he had forgiven her for her tactlessness. But Miriam's presence rooted her to the spot and she faced him, motionless, hoping desperately he would see in her eyes something of what she longed to tell him.

She took a deep breath to steady her voice.

'Lady Aylward called to see you,' she said formally, 'and as I wasn't expecting you back until tomorrow . . .'

'I thought I would stay the night and wait for your return,' Miriam put in pleasantly. 'I only need your signature, Piers—those legal documents we discussed last time we met.'

Piers' mouth narrowed into a thin line. She had wanted money, hadn't she? Cressida recalled. She should never have let Miriam win her round in this way, and should have sent her packing, but Miriam had got her way before Cressida had had time to act. The woman was a witch, weaving spells to get others to do her bidding. Thank goodness Piers had come back—no chance of holding the party now, and no one need ever be any the wiser.

Cressida felt as though a great load had been lifted from her shoulders, and her step took on an added lightness as she crossed the room to the doorway.

'I'll leave you to discuss your business,' she said, turning her back on Miriam to disguise the expression in her eyes as she smiled up at Piers.

'I'll see you later,' he said to her quietly, his own face serious and giving nothing away. Then, more softly still, 'She hasn't upset you, has she?'

Cressida shook her head, swept by a wave of gladness that Piers had thought to consider *her* feelings . . . then stopped as she was about to shut the door behind her. 'Will you still be staying the night, or shall I say goodbye, Lady Aylward?' She hoped the 'goodbye' sounded definite enough and final enough to scotch once and for all the party idea. Goodbye meant goodbye.

'You won't mind if I stay, will you, Piers?' Miriam opened her eyes wide and fixed them in mock helplessness on his stony face. 'It's rather late for a woman on her own to start looking for a room. I promise I won't be a nuisance—you needn't see me again. I'll even go before breakfast if that will make you happy.'

Piers shrugged impatiently.

'It doesn't matter to me one way or the other. I'll be away myself first thing. I only came back for my passport.'

Passport! Cressida's heart fell. He was going away again so soon, and abroad too! Were they never to have any time together to try and strengthen the frail bonds of their relationship? It was becoming increasingly hard to recapture the magic of that afternoon by the sea. The memory of that long, lovely embrace was receding ever further from her mind. Perhaps he was regretting it after all, now he had had time to think.

But Cressida knew she must hide her disappointment from Miriam's prying gaze.

'I'll say goodnight, then,' she said, and closed the door quietly behind her before making her way back to the kitchen and the mountain of washing-up Miriam had left. She was almost glad of the monumental task awaiting her. It would at least give her time to collect her thoughts.

'At last.'

Piers' voice was grim as he stormed into the kitchen to find her. Cressida began to speak, but thought better of it and merely pulled out a chair for him to slump into while she finished putting the last of the dishes away. Better let him simmer down. What had gone on in the Boudoir was none of her business—and the fact that he needed his passport hinted at possible difficulties at his publishers', too. He needed tranquillity, not a torrent of words and emotions.

'Coffee?' she enquired quietly. She could do with another cup herself—the last few hours hadn't been the calmest she had ever known.

Piers nodded. 'Thanks,' he said briefly, his thoughts elsewhere. His hands clenched tensely on his knee and he leapt up to go prowling round the room like a caged animal—a wolf, Cressida thought, or a tiger, solitary and brooding.

'Oh, Cressida—that woman! She knows just how to get me on the raw. Do you know what she said . . .?'

He came to a halt in front of her and grasped her shoulders, pinioning her arms to her sides.

'She actually suggested . . .' His eyes raked her fiercely from head to toe, and for a moment Cressida wondered whether he were angry with her, too . . . but what could she have done? She had been powerless to resist Miriam's demands. Something of what she was thinking must have shown on her face, for at last his expression softened.

'No—never mind . . . let's forget her.'

He released his grip only to clasp her more tightly to him, resting his cheek on her hair. At last, Cressida exulted, moulding her body to his—at last, and he hasn't forgotten, and he does still want me.

But where was Miriam? The last thing Cressida wanted was for Piers' sly sister-in-law to come and find them. Cressida pressed her hands against his chest and leant back to look up at him.

'Miriam—Lady Aylward? Where is she now? Has she gone?'

Piers barked a harsh laugh. 'Not her—not while she can get free board and lodging out of me.'

'She won't come and find us?'

'No—she's gone up to her room. She said she would leave first thing, but you can never tell with her.' He paused with a frown. 'If there's mischief to be made, she'll hang around long enough to make it . . she didn't upset you in any way, did she?'

Cressida wound her arms round his neck and smiled her reassurance. 'Not a bit—she even cooked supper for the two of us.' No need to mention the madcap scheme for the party. That was obviously a non-starter now. Best to forget the whole thing and put it down to experience, and she thanked her lucky stars that Piers had arrived in time to prevent her succumbing totally to Miriam's wiles.

'What about the coffee?' she murmured as the machine hissed to an aromatic silence. She was unable to do anything about it, imprisoned as she was in his arms.

'Mmm.' His hand felt for her chin and raised it, cupping it firmly as his lips came down on hers. This kiss was different, not just a kiss of tender exploration and delight at her response, but with a flutter almost of apprehension, Cressida knew from the fierce searching of his mouth that he wanted her, needed her with an almost animal urgency—maybe to assuage the bitterness Miriam's arrival had aroused in him.

Without warning he released her and strode over to the door, turning to her with outstretched hand in an imperious invitation.

'Leave that.' He nodded towards the coffee. 'Come to the study—we can't stay here.'

He stood watching her hungrily as she came towards him, and she felt her whole body tremble as she passed before him into the corridor. There was an expression deep in the gold-glinting eyes she hadn't seen before—fierce, predatory almost—and for a moment she almost felt afraid. It was as though she were a prize fought for and dominated by this descendant of an ancient Viking raider. The civilising legacy of past generations of Aylwards was momentarily wiped out by the primitive passion blazing under those dark brows.

'Cressida.'

His voice was hoarse with undisguised desire, and even from the other side of the room she could sense the turbulent instincts coiled like a spring within his body only waiting for a sign from her to be released in an overwhelming surge.

Her breathing became fast and shallow but she forced her eyes to meet his levelly as she walked slowly towards him, knowing she must meet him on equal terms, as a woman responding to a man, and not as slave surrending to her master.

Even so, he made no move to come to her but waited, gloating over her overt acceptance of his tacitly offered invitation. At last she had crossed the seemingly endless space between them and she stood before him, motionness but for the quickening of her breath. Piers smiled almost triumphantly as he took in the rapid rise and fall of her breast.

'Come,' he said shortly, and pulled her to him with a savagery that made Cressida gasp. There was no tenderness in him now. The gentleness with which he had embraced her in the grassy hollow was all gone, to be replaced by a tigerish ferocity which almost shocked her by its unexpectedness.

Why, Cressida thought wildly, why is he doing this to me—what have I done to him to deservc this? But, even as the thought whirled through her brain, her treacherous instincts were responding to the onslaught of his passion with an intoxicated fervour. All her womanly arts were called up from the very depths of her being to pleasure him as he—and she could no longer pretend otherwise—was pleasuring her.

He sank into the big leather armchair, dragging her after him so that she almost fell across his hard, demanding body. There was no longer any doubt about how much he desired her, no way he was going to be denied. She was in his power, utterly, and to resist would be useless, even had she wanted to.

A moan broke from Cressida's parted lips as Piers thrust his hand beneath her shirt, pulling it off roughly over her head. She felt the straps of her bra slip down her arms as the garment was swiftly undone, and her jeans being unzipped . . . then, with a half-stifled groan of release, Piers bent his head to her breast, burying his face in the firm flesh as she arched her back in an instinctive response to the touch of his roaming hands and searing lips.

A lightning shaft of naked desire struck through the very core of her body as together they slid to the floor, Cressida spreadeagled beneath the crushing weight of the man she had once thought so detached and self-controlled. But he was not self-controlled now. What fires had lain smouldering under that seemingly cool exterior—fires that she, Cressida, had been the woman to set ablaze here . . . now.

She smiled tremulously up at him as she eased her hands under his shirt, undoing the buttons one by one with a sensuous, teasing slowness that inflamed his questing lips once more. She let her fingers wander over his body, relishing the feel of the hard muscles tensed to the touch of her caresses.

A primitive cry was wrung from the lips now pressed again, fiercely and painfully, to her bruised mouth. Piers raised himself a little above her, gazing at her with a burning hunger which he slaked by drinking in every line of her face and body as though she might disappear from his sight. He brushed his hand lightly across her breasts, which swelled against him in an agonised wave of sensuality, and his fingers cupped their fullness as, with a laugh of delight, his lips closed on the hard, aching peaks of desire.

Ecstasy closed her eyes against the intrusive shapes of their surroundings as she thrust against him in urgent acceptance. His whole body sought her in ever-increasing fervour until it seemed the whole world vanished round them, sucking them into a whirlpool of passion which spun them round in an erupting explosion of light, and Cressida felt herself falling, falling into space, through time itself until there was nothing left, only her and Piers . . .

'Oh, my love.'

Cressida turned within the circle of his embrace, bruised and shaken by the violence of their lovemaking. She could hardly believe what had happened, but the weight of Piers' head on her shoulder told her she wasn't dreaming. She moved her arm to cradle him to her, lifting her head a little so that she could kiss him softly and tenderly now, their passion slaked and bodies exhausted. But there was an ache at the back of Cressida's mind, something that took the edge off the joy thrilling through her—what was it?

'Oh!'

The distress in her voice roused Piers from his own blissful state of semi-consciousness.

'Cressida? What's wrong? I haven't hurt you, have I? You're not angry or . . . I thought . . .'

The curve of her lips against his cheek reassured him, and she tightened her arms round him possessively.

'You're going away again. Do you really have to?'

Her tone was anguished and Piers raised himself slowly on to his elbow to gaze tenderly into her face, smoothing back the tumbled hair.

'Does it mean so much to you, my love?'

Cressida nodded mutely, her eyes fixed hungrily on his

'I didn't know, then, that this would happen.' He smiled, covering her with more kisses, one finger tracing the line of her breast.

She caught hold of his hand and lifted it to her mouth.

'Can't you change your plans? Wait at least a few days?'

Piers frowned worriedly. 'I don't think I can—it's all been fixed. Things to do with the book—interviews with people. It'd be very difficult . . .'

Cressida sighed. 'I guess I'll have to take second

place, then. I . . .'

'Not second place, never.' Piers pulled her to him again. 'I'll cancel it all, if you like, and stay here. You only have to say.'

Cressida's heart lifted, but she knew such a request would be the first step to disaster. It was enough to know he was prepared to do it for her.

'No——' She shook her head. 'Just ring me when you can, and come back as quickly as possible, won't you?'

For answer he rose slowly to his feet and drew her up to him, enfolding her in his arms. Then, without another word, he wrapped his jacket round her bare shoulders and led her though the darkened house to her room.

CHAPTER TEN

IT WAS the dawn chorus that woke Cressida, and with waking came an ineffable sense of loss which flooded through her as she reached across the empty space beside her. She buried her face in the pillow still tinged with the faint aroma of his skin. Did he always make his departures before daybreak, Cressida wondered, and where was he now? Was he thinking of her as she was longing for him?

She rolled over on to her back, linking her hands behind her head, and gazed up in a vain attempt to imprint the image of his face on the white expanse of the ceiling. A kind of slumber enveloped her again as she etched each line of his features on to her mind, and she drifted between sleep and wakefulness, half-dreaming, half remembering with a mixture of elation and misery until it was time to get up to face the day alone. . . and Miriam!

Miriam!

The very thought of her presence somewhere in the house was enough to rouse Cressida to instant activity, for one thing was certain—she would not have kept to her promise to leave first thing. The very idea was laughable. Miriam was one who liked her creature comforts above everything else.

Cressida struggled out of bed and pulled on her clothes, which someone—Piers—had placed in a neat pile on the chair. She paused only long enough to check her face in the mirror for any tell-tale sign of Piers' fierce kisses that had raked her skin only hours before. She felt that every inch of her body must be glowing as a beacon of their passion, but, rather to her disappointment, there seemed to be nothing out of the ordinary about her appearance.

And now she must face Miriam, and above all things keep her cool. She must not give her any weapon to use against Piers in the future, and there was something she must find out before Miriam came downstairs.

Cressida opened her door and slipped quietly into the main part of the house, listening intently. Nothing stirred. She let herself into the study and glanced round anxiously. There wasn't a sign of what had happened there the evening before. Piers' clothing had vanished, the rugs were straight and it looked as though no one had ever disturbed its masculine orderliness. Cressida sighed with a pang of regret, then smiled to herself. Trust Piers to see to everything. The tidy mind at work again. She paused and gazed round, hoping but not really expecting, some message, however small, left for her . . . but there was nothing.

A sound from upstairs brought her back to earth. Miriam was around. Cressida allowed herself just one more regretful glance at the armchair before she closed the door behind her and hurried off to the kitchen.

'Did you sleep well?' she enquired brightly of the bleary-eyed Miriam who groped her way to the table some time later and flopped on to a chair. She was obviously a night person, judging from her frail appearance. 'Shall I make some toast—a fried egg, perhaps? I've finished mine . . . it's a lovely day, isn't it?'

Miriam shuddered. 'Nothing to eat, darling—just a cup of coffee.'

Cressida grinned and poured her a cup.

Miriam raised her heavy eyes to Cressida's. She looked quite different without all that make-up, younger and even rather vulnerable. For a moment Cressida felt almost sorry for her, until she remembered all the anguish she had caused Piers and the disaster she and her husband had brought to the Priory. Although . . . Cressida smiled to herself while her back was turned . . . if they hadn't made such depredations on the family's finances, she, Cressida, wouldn't be here now, and wouldn't have spent last night in Piers' arms . . .

'So what about it, then?'

Miriam's voice was stronger, now, restored by the coffee.

'What about what?' Cressida regarded her, puzzled.

'The party, of course. You can't have forgotten already, an efficient girl like you.'

For a moment Cressida wondered whether Miriam was actually jealous of her position here—no, it was too ridiculous. She ignored the gibe, but before she could go onto dismiss the idea, Miriam continued, 'Now that Piers had gone away for a while—he has gone, darling, hasn't he? He's not lurking around the house somewhere?'

Cressida shook her head. 'Not as far as I know. I didn't hear him go, but I'm sure he's not around. He's usually had his breakfast by now.'

With a slight lift of one eyebrow and a shadow of a smile, Miriam forced Cressida to meet her gaze, but Cressida's eyes never wavered. She was determined to give nothing away. Miriam shrugged thin shoulders beneath the elegant dressing-gown. So be it, she seemed to say.

'So there we are, then,' she drawled. 'The coast is clear, *n'est-ce pas*?' She got slowly to her feet and stretched, catlike. Cressida could almost imgaine the scarlet nails shooting out to dig themselves into her flesh as a hand was laid on her arm.

'Now, I don't want you to worry about a single thing,' Miriam reassured Cressida silkily. 'You get on with whatever it is you do and leave all the details to me. I thrive on this sort of thing—positively thrive, believe me.'

Cressida looked at her dubiously. She knew in her heart of hearts that this party notion was all wrong, but Miriam seemed to have a way of getting past all her defences, and maybe if she let her have her own way and they got the party over before Piers returned, he need never know. And if, as Miriam seemed to think, it was a success, the publicity couldn't do any harm, just so long as it was the right kind of publicity. It was up to her to see that it was.

'I'll get off as soon as I'm ready,' Miriam told her. 'No point in hanging on here now. I've got thousands of people to see—suppose we say next Saturday?'

'Saturday?' Cressida's jaw fell open. 'So soon? Surely you won't be able to arrange everything by then, not if it's to be as big an event as you suggested?'

'You don't know me, darling.' Miriam's mouth curved in a self-satisfied smile. 'Saturday is ages away, positively ages. I could fix it for tonight if I had to.'

In spite of all her reservations, Cressida couldn't help being impressed, just as she was by the speed with which Miriam dressed, put on her make-up and got ready to leave, and all before Mary Bryant arrived.

'The fewer people who know, the better, don't you agree? Just in case it gets back to dear old Piers.' Miriam paused, one hand on the door of her smart little car. 'You don't have any idea when he's coming back, I suppose?'

'No, I don't. All he said was that he was going

abroad. I don't even know where.'

Cressida was pleased by the evenness of tone she managed to produce. Surely, whatever Miriam's suspicions of what might have gone on between herself and Piers, she could have no actual proof that their relationship was anything other than that of colleagues and maybe friends, too?

But Miriam only had one thing on her mind now, and even while she was getting into the car Cressida could tell by her slight frown and preoccupied expression that she was already mentally back in London, fixing, telephoning, wheedling . . .

She turned the car in a swift, tight circle and waved once at Cressida.

'See you Friday, I expect,' she called—and shot off down the drive, leaving Cressida staring, fascinated in spite of herself, after her. What a woman! Slowly she turned and went back into the Priory, catching as she did so the eye of one of the Aylwards staring down at her. Sir Thomas it was, one of the eighteenth-century ancestors, and it seemed to her that he looked more disapproving then usual.

'I know,' Cressida muttered. 'I know it's wrong. I know Piers won't like it, but she gave me no option. As they all say, she's got a will of her own.'

'Talking to yourself, Cress? That won't do, you know.'

Mary appeared from the direction of the back door, duster in hand.

'Was that Lady Aylward's car that passed me in the drive? She was going so fast I couldn't get more than a glimpse, but it certainly looked like her at the wheel.'

She rubbed energetically at a spot on the long oak table.

Cressida nodded. 'She came yesterday evening to see

Piers about something, and as it was late by the time he came back she wheedled her way into staying the night. She . . .' Should she say anything about the proposed party? Mary's sharp eyes flicked towards her, waiting for the end of the sentence.

'She said to leave the room with the bed made up in case she had to come back,' Cressida finished lamely, hating to have to deceive Mary. 'Oh, and Piers has gone away again, and doesn't know for how long.'

She knew she must keep the party a secret. Mary would try to dissuade her, but the die had been cast now and the only thing she could do was to make sure it went off as quietly as possible and above all tidy away all signs that anything untoward had been going on before Piers did come back.

Cressida tried, mostly unsuccessfully, to put all thoughts of Miriam and her plans out of her mind during the next few days, throwing herself and her energies into her own work and putting the finishing touches to the show-rooms and, when she had a quiet moment, letting the memories of that last night with Piers flood back in a tidal wave of longing.

She would wander out into the Elizabethan garden when she got the chance, for there among the plants so lovingly tended by Piers she felt closest to him. She dwelt on every miraculous sea-change which had transformed the cold, withdrawn man who had brought her out here that first afternoon, so long ago it seemed now, into the passionate lover who had held her in his arms and swept her away with him to an unimaginable ecstasy. She hugged the memory to herself as she tried to recapture just a shadow of the bliss they had shared . . . and, please God, would share again.

With an overwhelming ache of desire Cressida gazed at the little plants at her feet and knelt to pick a small sprig of forget-me-not which she cupped gently in her hand before tucking it inside her blouse.

Just to remember him by, she told herself, almost ashamed by the sentimental gesture, and knowing she didn't really need a flower to remind her of Piers, but it was a comfort to feel the little flower against her skin.

As the week wore on, Cressida became increasingly edgy, unable to settle to anything until Mary, finding her following her round the house from room to room, couldn't stand it any longer.

'For goodness' sake, Cressida, love—whatever's got into you? You're like the proverbial cat on hot bricks. It's not like you to be so fidgety.' She smiled kindly. 'He always comes back, you know.'

Cressida's flush must have given her feelings away, and she longed more than ever to be able to confide everything—Miriam's plans as well as her feelings for Piers—but something still held her back and she just looked helplessly at her friend.

'Come over on Sunday—have lunch with Alan and me,' Mary suggested. 'It's not good for you to be here by yourself, rattling round in this great place. You need company.'

If only she could, but Sunday . . .? Even if Miriam's friends had gone by lunch time, which was very unlikely, Cressida could picture only too clearly the chaos they would have left behind them. She hedged, muttering something unconvincing about last-minute jobs to see to, but Mary wasn't to be put off so lightly.

'Ring me tomorrow,' she told Cressida cheerfully as she was leaving after lunch on the Friday. 'That'll be time enough—and try to make it, won't you?'

Mary's departure had removed the last comforting bulwark between normality and Miriam's arrival, and Cressida suddenly felt very alone and very vulnerable.

All her instincts told her to run away—she could go home and spend the weekend with her parents—but she knew she must stay and keep a watch over the Priory. It was her responsibility, after all, and maybe she was letting the whole thing get out of proportion. Maybe there would only be a gathering of a few rich and influential people who really could be useful in providing the right sort of publicity. She mustn't be influenced by the stories of what had gone on in Hugo's time—Miriam might have changed.

But her optimism was short-lived. The arrival during Friday afternoon of a vanload of wine, vodka, whisky . . . almost the whole contents of an off-licence, it seemed to Cressida, along with hundreds of glasses, put paid to the hope that the gathering would be small and select.

'Expecting company, love?' the van-driver grinned as he proffered the slip of paper for her sign. 'Enough here for a quite a do, isn't there?'

'Quite a do.' Cressida echoed faintly, taking in the vast quantity of cases stacked in the Great Hall. 'Sale or return, I take it?'

The man laughed. 'There won't be much to return, not if it's like the old days.' Cressida's heart sank. 'You weren't here then?' He drew in his breath and shook his head at the memory. 'My, but they had some wild times—good for business, mind, but the stories that I've heard . . . you wouldn't credit some of them.'

Cressida began to feel sick. Maybe it would be different this time—it certainly would if she had anything to do with it, though what she could do once Miriam and her friends got the bit between their teeth, she couldn't imagine.

She was still gazing at the stacks of bottles when the sound of an approaching car made her move to the doorway. Miriam.

She leapt out. 'Is that the drink?' she asked, without so much as a word of greeting. 'Everything I ordered?'

'I should imagine so,' Cressida returned gloomily. 'I've never seen so much in one place, outside of a shop. Will you—we—really need all this?'

Miriam's gay laugh echoed round the old walls. 'All the old crowd are coming . . . you wait.' She patted Cressida's arm. 'It'll be a party to remember, you'll see. They're a good lot, they'll see you have some fun.' She paused and stepped back from Cressida, frowning critically at her appearance.

'We'll have to do something about you, though.' She walked all round her, staring up at her face and undisciplined hair. 'Have you got a party dress? Something rather dashing—you are in charge here, after all, and you want to make the most of the chance to put the old place on the map, don't you? You'll need to stand out.'

Stand out? How could she stand out among the fashionable crowd Miriam was expecting? Even Miriam in everyday clothes put her to shame. Cressida shook her head helplessly.

'I haven't anything really suitable—it never crossed my mind that I'd need that sort of outfit when I came here.' The lace blouse and ankle-length taffeta skirt which were her current party-going gear were at home in Kent. And somehow she didn't think they were quite what Miriam had in mind. Miriam was still frowning as she turned to prowl round the cases of bottles, flicking them with her red nails as she mentally ticked off the contents, and mesmerising Cressida again by her mercurial movements.

'Of course!' She snapped her fingers and slewed round to face Cressida with a movement too impulsive to give her time to disguise the glint of what looked like real malice on the sharp features. Cressida recoiled—what was she up to now? 'Wait here,' Miriam ordered her. 'I won't be long—if it's still there.'

She darted away and Cressida could hear the rapid clack of her heels fading away as she ran up the staircase in search of . . . what? Beneath the severe gaze of Piers' ancestors, she waited in powerless apprehension for her return. If only it were all over . . .

'Here you are, darling—we had a fancy dress ball one year and this was a real sensation. Annabel, a dear friend of mine, wore it . . . about your size, too . . .' Her lips curved at some private memory as she thrust the garment into Cressida's unwilling hands. 'Come on, let's see . . .'

Cressida held it against herself and peered down to judge the effect. It seemed a very flimsy affair, the bodice almost non-existent between the low neck and the high waist. Not her style at all. There was something about it that seemed vaguely familiar, and at the same time worrying.

'I don't think . . .' she began doubtfully, but Miriam brushed her words aside with a gesture of impatience.

'You haven't anything else, have you?' Cressida shook her head. 'Then go and try it on—I'll be along in a moment.'

It was with considerable reluctance that Cressida took off her clothes and prepared to put on the dress. As a garment, it was very pretty—creamy-white and made of some silky material which would catch the light as the wearer moved. Even so, there was something about it that didn't exactly repel her, but which made Cressida feel *she* shouldn't be wearing it. Better to stick out like a sore thumb in her frilled blouse and pleated skirt . . . but Miriam would be sure to get her way in this, as in everything else. She was so dominating, Cressida felt powerless to resist her.

With a resigned sigh Cressida slipped the dress over her head and eased it down her body.

'I can't wear this,' she gasped out loud, appalled. She didn't need a full-length mirror to tell her what the effect must be. She had realised the bodice was cut low, but not this low! A bra was out of the question; the top half of her breasts were totally uncovered, moulded and supported by the tight, high waist. She just couldn't wear anything so revealing. As she moved to the mirror on the chest of drawers the silky folds moved sensuously against her limbs, reinforcing her utter distaste of the dress. It had been made and worn with one idea only—to catch the eye and rouse the desire of every man who saw it and the woman wearing it. She couldn't contemplate appearing dressed like this before a houseful of strangers.

Even as her hands were grasping the skirt to lift it over her head, a perfunctory knock on the door warned her of Miriam's arrival, and before she could call out, the other woman had appeared in her bedroom.

'Oh, yes!' The brown eyes sparkled with approval. Miriam marched over to Cressida and rearranged the folds. 'Oh, yes,' she repeated, 'it might have been made for you. What a brilliant inspiration that was!'

Cressida took a deep breath. She must be firm.

'I can't wear it. I'd rather just put on what I've got . . . and in any case, you don't need me there at all.' She clutched desperately at this straw of hope. 'You can run that party without me.'

Miriam's expression changed. The brown eyes became hard stones and her mouth narrowed into a scarlet line of menace. Cressida stepped back, almost frightened by the abrupt transformation not only on

Miriam's face but in the atmosphere.

'You will wear it, my darling—and you'll be a sensation, I promise you.'

It sounded more like a threat. 'But I don't want . . .'

'What you want is beside the point. I . . . want . . . you . . . to.' She punctuated each word with a stab at Cressida's bare arm.

'You have no right to make me do anything.' Cressida drew herself up to her full height. 'I have no intention of wearing this just because you tell me to.'

A nasty smile spread over Miriam's face. 'I don't think you quite understand, darling. I want you to wear it and you are going to wear it . . . otherwise . . .' She moved closer, almost touching Cressida. 'Otherwise I shall tell your precious Piers that the party was all your idea. "I tried my best to dissuade her, but she positively insisted . . . I knew she couldn't be trusted, but you wouldn't listen to me." Something like that.'

Cressida paled. She had no doubt that the threat was no idle one, nor of the strength of Miriam's powers of persuasion. But why was it so important to her that Cressida wear the dress? There was some devious scheme behind her insistence, she knew.

Cressida tried to think sensibly. Her main responsibility was to Piers and the Priory, and if that meant attending Miriam's party and wearing the awful dress, it was perhaps only a small sacrifice to make. Better than Piers thinking she was behind it all, and she had no illusions about Miriam's ability to make the lie sound convincing.

Slowly she turned back to face Miriam. 'Very well. I'll come to your party and wear the dress, if it does mean so much to you.'

'Oh, it does—it really does. I knew you'd see sense in the end.' Miriam grinned triumphantly. 'And you'll let me fix your hair?'

Cressida nodded. Useless to try to prevent her.

'Good.' Miriam almost purred with satisfaction. 'Now, I must get back to my telephoning. It'll all be worth it, you'll see. The publicity's going to be fabulous.'

So's the telephone bill, Cressida thought in mounting alarm. Still, there was nothing she could do about that or anything else, except pray the whole thing would pass off with the minimum of havoc and no actual disaster.

CHAPTER ELEVEN

CRESSIDA woke next morning with a sinking feeling that the constant stream of delivery vans bringing food, lighting and music equipment—and even more drink—did nothing to allay. She wandered round the house like a lost soul, constantly meeting friends of Miriam's who had arrived early to lend a hand with what with dread she overheard one of them describe as 'the party to end all parties'.

Thank God Piers was out of the country. She had heard nothing from him, which surely meant he was safely beyond reach of any means of communication in some remote part of the world. And may he remain there, too, she thought fervently, even though his absence brought on waves of heartache whenever she called to mind that last night before his departure, the feel of his lips, his body . . . no, those memories must be put into cold storage.

She retreated to her room during the afternoon, but kept watch on the courtyard, unable, in spite of her misgivings, to restrain her curiosity as hordes of smart, noisy people kept arriving in a fleet of cars as flashy and expensive-looking as their owners.

Eventually, though, the time came when she could no longer postpone changing. The only thought to give her any comfort was that no one there would know her, have the slighest interest in her or be likely to meet her again. She had also found a shawl, lacy and quite pretty, among her own clothes, and she would cover herself with this when the time came to make her appearance.

Miriam had told her when she would come to arrange her hair, and bang on time she hurried into Cressida's bedroom without so much as a warning knock.

She looked stunning, even Cressida had to admit that, in a black strapless dress which set off the creamy whiteness of her skin and dark chestnut hair to perfection. The large ruby on her finger flashed as she moved her hands up to Cressida's hair, twisting and pulling it to get the effect she wanted.

'That'll do very well,' she stated at last with satisfaction. 'Now, do your bit—this is all for publicity on *your* behalf, don't forget.' She held up a mirror for Cressida, who stared at the reflection of her tresses piled up on her head in elaborate glossy coils. Almost she didn't recognise herself, but she still felt just as apprehensive, and very lonely as she waited for the moment when she had to emerge to join the throng.

It was early yet, but even so the volume of noise from the thudding music competing with the din of all the shouting and laughter was already reaching an ear-splitting level.

Cressida need not have worried about her appearance. Among all the bare backs, shoulders and bosoms of the extremes of fashion sported by Miriam's guests, her own state of what she had thought of as semi-nudity seemed almost unremarkable. In fact, she decided as she pushed her way to a dark corner of the Great Hall to watch the scene unobserved, no one showed the least interest in her, nor did Miriam make any attempt to seek her out and introduce her to the influential people she had promised would be there. Clearly that had just been a ploy to get Cressida to agree to the party.

Where had they all come from, these brightly dressed and very noisy people, and had Miriam really charged them all for coming? The very thought of what all this must have cost made Cressida's mind reel. Who was going to pay for it? As she had told Miriam, there was hardly any money left in the fund Piers had arranged for her to draw on—certainly nothing adequate to settle even a fraction of the bills that would flow in after this evening. She suddenly felt quite ill as the whole thing began to fall into place—Miriam had planned the whole thing to get back at Piers . . . and she had fallen right into the trap.

She must get some air . . . try to think. She struggled to get through the press of people, coming up hard against the edge of the great oak table which was laden with bottles and glasses. Her way out was temporarily blocked by a red-faced middle-aged man who appeared out of the crowd beside her, close enough for her to smell the drink on his breath. He was perspiring heavily and leered at Cressida with bloodshot eyes which narrowed as they travelled slowly the length of her body, resting appreciatively on the exposed curve of her breast.

'Very interesting dress,' he drawled, thrusting his face into hers. 'Very shapely . . .' His hands sketched some graphic curves before reaching to caress the bare flesh of her upper arm beneath the tight, puffed sleeve.

The face got closer and the hand lower, and Cressida had to repress a shudder as she tried to back away. She raised her glass quickly to make a barrier between them and took a large gulp of wine to steady herself. Then his attention was caught momentarily by a voice behind him and Cressida took the opportunity to make her escape, pushing hard through the crowd of people between her and the invisible door through which Piers had made his first entrance, then, at last and with considerable relief, she reached the comparative tranquillity of the dining-room. There was no one there and she sank on to the chair at the head of the table, all her instincts crying out to leave the party altogether—no one would miss her—but an overriding sense of duty told her she must stay to make sure none of the excesses of past occasions that had been so darkly hinted at took place this time, though what she could do to prevent them she had no idea. Nothing at all, if she were honest.

And always her mind returned to the appalling cost of it all. What was she going to do—and what was Piers going to say? There was no way she could hide it from him now, whenever he came back, for the more she thought of it, the more sure she was that Miriam would never have asked all these people to pay to come here tonight. At least she had a few minutes' peace to try to work something out.

However, she was not to remain undisturbed for long. Her heart sank as she heard footsteps—familiar, clacking footsteps approaching, too purposeful to belong to anyone but Miriam.

'Ah, there you are,' she addressed Cressida crossly. 'What are you doing, skulking in here? That's no way to behave when I've gone to all this trouble for you.'

She hurried back to the door, calling to someone outside in the passage. 'It's all right, she's in here.'

A man came in to join her. A camera was slung round his neck and the lines of his handsome face were set in a sulky pout at having been dragged away from the fun.

'Over there, I thought.' Miriam pointed towards the wall behind Cressida, totally ignoring her. The man nodded uninterestedly and stood in an exaggerated pose of boredom, clearly waiting for some sort of action to begin.

'Come on, get up. We haven't got all night.'

Cressida stared at Miriam in astonishement. 'Are you talking to me?'

'Who else, darling? Get your act together, for goodness' sake. You said you wanted publicity, so I've arranged it. Damian here is waiting to take your picture, aren't you, Damian?'

Damian grunted and stared, unimpressed, at Cressida.

'You don't want pictures of me,' Cressida protested. 'The Priory, I thought you meant . . .'

'No one's interested in that—bricks and mortar are dead.' Miriam tapped her fingernail irritably on the polished table. 'But you in the Lady Maria dress with the real lady in the background . . . then some shots of the party. That'll bring them in. Human interest, that's what peope like.' She laughed loudly.

Lady Maria! Of course! No wonder Cressida's dress had seemed familiar. She turned slowly, almost unwillingly, to look at the painting on the wall behind her, and the gentle curve of Lady Maria's bosom modestly clothed in the flowing white dress—by comparison Cressida's costume was a gross caricature. She could imagine only too well how the contrast would be pointed up by the editors of whatever papers Damian was intending to send his photographs to—it wouldn't be *Country Life*, that was for certain. If publicity material like that brought in any visitors, they certainly wouldn't be the kind that Cressida had been aiming to attract. The whole idea was preposterous as well as distasteful. She stood up, but stayed resolutely by her chair.

'No. Thanks for the idea, Miriam, but that sort of publicity is not what we want.'

Menace gleamed in Miriam's eyes. 'You have no choice in the matter darling.'

It was at that moment that Cressida finally realised just how much Hugo's widow hated the Aylwards—and Piers. She, herself, was only a pawn in the game Miriam was playing to get her own back . . . but for what? The fact that she hadn't inherited the Priory after Hugo's death? Or was it just that she was malicious enough to enjoy causing as much misery as she could for its own sake?

Miriam gave her no time to decide what action to take. She pulled at Cressida's arm and dragged her over towards the wall to face Lady Maria's gentle gaze.

'If you don't do just as you're told,' she hissed savagely, 'I'll tell your precious Piers the party was your idea. I warned you before . . . see what he says then.'

'He'd never believe you.'

'Do you want to take the risk?' Miriam fixed Cressida with a threatening stare. 'At best he'd despise you for giving in to his wicked sister-in-law; at worst . . .' She shrugged, and Cressida didn't have to have the rest explained. She could see it all: the blame, the disgust . . . This way, if only Piers stayed away long enough, he would never see the photos.

'Very well, then.' Cressida's voice was cold. 'Where shall I stand?'

Reluctantly she allowed herself to be pulled and pushed by Miriam and Damian, hating every minute of it, hating the feel of their hands adjusting her dress to accentuate its revealing lines to the maximum and to achieve the most voluptuous pose they could devise.

'You've got quite a talent for it,' Miriam sneered as she and Damian were about to leave. 'Once Piers has decided to dispense with your services you might find yourself a new career as a Page Three model.'

She waited until Damian had gone, then added her parting shot from the doorway, her face hard and vicious.

'For make no mistake about it, once Piers knows what's been going on here you can say goodbye to all your hopes of becoming Lady Aylward . . . oh, yes, darling,' she went on, seeing Cressida's appalled expression. 'I knew what you were up to from the start, and I can tell you, you're not going to get your greedy little hands on the Priory, or its owner, not if I have anything to do with it.'

She smiled triumphantly, and then she was gone, leaving Cressida too stunned and wretched to do anything except slump back into her chair. Vague notions of trying to sabotage the film flitted through her head, but she knew the very idea was hopeless. Why did Miriam hate her so much, and why had she, Cressida, allowed herself to be manipulated so weakly.

She took another gulp of wine, knowing it wasn't a good idea. She must keep a clear head, but she was almost past caring what happened.

More footsteps in the corridor put all thoughts of Miriam and her machinations temporarily from her mind. She stood up and pulled the dress as high as it would go, draping her shawl over her bare shoulders. She listened—it wasn't Miriam this time, the feet were too slow and shambling. As they approached, she thought she heard something suspiciously like a hiccup, but then, to her relief, they seemed to go past the door.

Cressida hesitated as she wondered what to do next. She must find somewhere else to sit for the rest of the evening—somewhere quiet where she would be undisturbed to give her time to try to sort out her apparently hopeless situation. Piers' study might be safe—but even as she moved towards the door the red-faced man whose unwelcome attentions she had escaped from earlier lurched over the threshold, grinning stupidly at her.

He was clutching a bottle, and, seeing Cressida's empty glass, stumbled across the floor towards her.

'Have a drink. Good wine, this—good ol' Miriam, always trust her to get the best.'

Breathing hard with concentration, he slopped out some wine in the vague direction of her glass, spilling some down her dress.

Sorry about that.' He laughed loudly and reached out to make ineffectual brushing movements against the folds of her skirt.

'That's all right.' Cressida moved sharply backwards, her voice cool with distaste.

'All right, is it? I'll say it's all right.' With another giggle, obscene coming from a man of his age, he straightened up, his eyes travelling slowly up her body and finally coming to rest on the curves half-hidden beneath Cressida's protective shawl.

'Saw you in the other room, didn't I? Grand dress, that—strange, but very fetching.'

His hand shot out towards her, aiming to pull the shawl away to give him a better view.

'Kindly leave me alone.' Cressida twisted away from him, but in doing so only managed to achieve what her unwelcome admirer had been hoping for. The shawl slipped from her shoulders and remained firmly in his grasp. He ran his tongue over his lips, unable to tear his lecherous gaze away from her semi-naked breasts and blocking her escape-route to the open doorway.

She knew if she made any move forward he would make a grab for her, so she began to back away, hoping to get the table between them before he realised what she was doing.

'I can see what you're doing—leading me on, aren't you?'

Before Cressida could get away he lunged forward with surprising agility and clutched her round her waist, then bent his head to press his lips to the tight cleavage exposed by the low neckline. Cressida gritted her teeth and pushed against him with all her strength.

'Get away, you horrible man. How dare you?'

But he only laughed. 'Playing hard to get, are you?' He ran his hands down her back, fumbling and insistent till she felt physically sick, but the more she struggled, the tighter he held her against him. It was useless. The only thing she could do was play along with him until she got her chance to escape, or they were interrupted. God, he was revolting!

He pulled her head towards him and tried to kiss her.

'Lovely girl,' he mumbled, trying to slip her hand inside her bodice. 'Lovely . . .'

Cressida had been so intent on coping with the man's disgusting attentions that Miriam, with Damian still in tow, had been able to enter the dining-room completely unobserved. The first Cressida knew of their presence was the click of Damian's camera, followed by Miriam's throaty chuckle.

'Harry, you naughty man—what have you been doing with our Cressida?'

'Lovely girl, Cress . . . Cressida.' Harry grinned at Miriam, who leaned against the wall, savouring every detail of the scene before her. The camera went on clicking while Cressida struggled to free herself, but Harry wasn't to be put off so easily.

'Come on—another kiss for Harry.'

Again he bent his head, and Cressida put her hands on his shoulders, preparing to give an almighty shove in a superhuman effort to get rid of him once and for all.

'Cressida!'

Like characters in a tableau, everyone froze, too

stunned to move.

'Piers . . . I—we—weren't expecting you back . . .'

'I can see that.' His lips curled in disgust.

Cressida's hands flew from Harry's shoulders with what, she realised too late, must look like a recoil of guilt. Fearfully she met Piers' gaze, grim and icy cold.

'What exactly is going on here?'

His voice was very quiet and even Miriam's laugh sounded forced.

'What does it look like, darling? We're having a party.'

Piers looked directly at Cressida, ignoring the others, his dark brows raised as he waited for her explanation. 'What have you got to say about it?'

What could she say? She spread her hands helplessly and felt a deep flush redden her face and neck, spreading down to her plunging neckline, and a streak of fear ran through her body. Cool and detached she had seen him, even angry after his interview with Miriam, but never like this. It was as though a volcano of burning ice were about to erupt, all the more frightening for being so rigorously under control . . . for the moment.

Miriam laughed again, a brittle sound which did nothing to ease the tension.

'Cressida's been great—helped me organise the whole thing, haven't you, darling?' Cressida swung towards her, horrified. 'And wait till you see the pictures Damian's taken—they'll do wonders for your publicity campaign. Have everyone flocking in—you'll see!'

'Is this true?'

Piers took a threatening step forward.

Cressida shook her head. 'No, of course not,' she asserted desperately. 'It wasn't like that at all—you must believe me.'

There was a short silence while Piers seemed to take in for the first time the revealing lines of Cressida's dress. His eyes dwelt appraisingly on the only too visible curves of her body, then he gave a quick, unbelieving glance at the portrait of Lady Maria Aylward on the wall behind her.

'I don't know why I should believe you.'

'Lovely dress . . . lovely girl . . .'

Harry had been silent all this time, his drink-fuddled brain working overtime to grasp what was going on. He'd slumped on to a chair and swivelled round now to leer again at Cressida.

'What's going on, anyway? Come on, don't mind him, whoever he is. We were having a good time . . .' He reached out to grab at her skirt.

'Oh, leave me alone . . .' Cressida's voice broke on a sob. She couldn't wait to hear any more, not Piers' accusations, nor Harry's suggestive comments and the sound of Miriam's mocking laughter followed her, mingling with the clamorous crescendo of music and laughter interspersed with the occasional shriek which assailed her ears as she approached the Great Hall. A quick glance through the doors confirmed her worst suspicions—had Piers also witnessed the Bacchanalian scenes before going in search of the instigators of those orgiastic goings-on? And he blamed her!

With a cry of despair drowned in the waves of sound echoing round the old walls, Cressida ran to her own room where she tore off the hateful dress and flung it into the corner. She pulled on an old pair of jeans and a sweater, hardly thinking what she was doing, and began piling her belongings into her suitcases. She couldn't stay here a moment longer—it was all over. Someone else could take over her job . . . Piers, Miriam, what did it matter?

All that did matter was to escape before she had to face Piers and his terrible rage again. She would simply leave everything and run, leaving no trace behind, no reason for her ever to have any further contact with the Priory or its owner.

There! She'd got everything in, and the cases fastened . . . if she could just get them out round the back, she would borrow the Old Ford and go to the Bryants'. Alan could bring the car back tomorrow by which time she would be well on the way home and away from Suffolk for ever. She paused in the doorway of her office and gave a last look round.

'Where do you think you're going?'

With a sigh of resignation—she might have known she would never make it—Cressida dropped her suitcase and leant wearily against the passage wall, registering with a bitter sense of irony that Piers was wearing the same old Aran sweater and cords he'd had on the first time she had seen him. She noticed, too, that his face was white and drawn, the anger behind every taut line of his features suppressed and all the more dangerous for that. Whatever had been said in the dining-room since her flight had done nothing to pacify him or persuade him she was not to blame.

'Come back in here—we don't want everyone to hear us.'

She followed him back into her office where he closed the door, taking up his stand with his back to it, effectively blocking off her escape.

All at once her legs threatened to give way under her, and she swayed, but Piers neither came to her aid nor showed the remotest glimmer of sympathy, and she determined not to give in to her weakness and give him any psychological advantage over her. She reached instead for the nearest chair and grasped its back for support before forcing her eyes to meet his levelly and candidly.

'I know how it must look,' Cressida told Piers quietly, 'and I blame myself for giving in to Miriam—Lady Aylward. It was weak and stupid . . .' She sighed. 'She said things . . . made threats . . . but I should have been strong enough to ignore them. I admit that and I'm deeply sorry.'

'And that obscene dress you were wearing? To say nothing of the choice little scene I interrupted? Don't tell me Miriam forced you into those. Not even my dear sister-in-law could devise threats to make you throw yourself into the arms of a man like that.' Piers took a step nearer, his eyes bright with scorn. 'You're nothing but a slut! You deceived me . . . you deceived us all. When I think . . .' He closed his eyes for a moment and clenched his hands into tight fists, beating impotently against his thighs.

The words of accusation stung like a whiplash and tears of hurt welled up in Cressida's eyes, spilling unheeded down her flushed cheeks. She bit her lip to stop it trembling.

'If you can think that of me, there's no point in my saying anything else.'

'How do I know what to think?' For the first time Cressida felt truly intimidated as he drew himself up to stare coldly down at her, as he called her to account for betraying his trust.

'You disgust me.' The words were barely audible, but they were uttered with such loathing that Cressida's arm shot up in an instinctive gesture of self-preservation, and she cringed back against the chair.

'Piers . . .'

There were shouts and a crash somewhere out in the courtyard, followed by shrieks of uncontrollable laughter.

Piers' eyes narrowed and his jaw tensed furiously. 'I'll

be back.' He flung himself out of the door and vanished.

There was no time to lose. She would leave the luggage—Mary and Alan would cope with it, she knew. She snatched up her small grip containing her money, and she slipped quitely out of the Priory and into the courtyard. There was chaos all round her and for once Cressida had cause to be glad, for no one would notice her in the press of cars and bodies. Somewhere among them she saw a tall figure, fair hair gleaming in the light from the windows, but he never saw Cressida as she kept in the shadow of the wall before running as fast as she could down the drive and out of the gate.

Somehow she got the Bryants' cottage, stumbling and exhausted, and begged them not to ask any questions but to let her stay there till the next morning.

'I'll write and tell you what's happened,' she promised Mary as she climbed into Alan's car the following morning, 'but I don't think I'll be back.'

Alan drove her to the station and reassured her that he would see to her things . . . and that was that. Episode closed. Goodbye Clarewood Priory, goodbye Byrants . . . goodbye Sir Piers Aylward.

'It didn't work out,' was all she told her surprised parents. 'I'll explain some time—but not now.'

In a valiant effort to keep her mind off the Priory, Cressida flung herself into as many activities as she could find. She got a temporary job and used up any spare time assisting in her mother's antiques market and helping out in the surgery—anything to stop her thinking about what she would have been doing at Clarewood and, much more difficult, about Piers.

There hadn't been a word from him. Alan Bryant had sent on her luggage, and that was it. Nothing. All her hard work during the past months might never have happened, and as for the rest . . .

Miriam must have used her wiles on Piers, too, persuading him that Cressida had been the sole inspiration behind the terrible party.

'Oh, for the best reasons, darling.' She could hear Miriam's plausible words only too plainly. 'She wanted all the publicity she could get, and—well . . . you know me . . .' with a widening of the brown eyes here, helpless and appealing ' . . . I can't resist a party, and I suppose it did get a bit out of hand. I did what I could, of course, but, well—she wasn't quite what the Priory needed, was she?'

Cressida could not really blame Piers for jumping to the wrong conclusions when he had come on that scene as he had, with her giving every appearance of enjoying that revolting man's embrace and wearing that dreadful dress. But surely, *surely* he could have been prepared to listen to her side of the story after all they had begun to mean to one another. That was what hurt most and what kept her awake during the long nights. After all he had said about Miriam, he had chosen to believe her.

As the date of the opening approached—if indeed that was still going ahead as planned . . . as *she* had planned—Cressida found it increasingly difficult even during the daytime to keep her thoughts away from the Priory. Who was in charge now? Had Miriam wheedled her way into her, Cressida's, job after all, or would Piers have swallowed his pride and taken over himself?

She hoped they would remember to collect the guide-books from Mr Prentice—oh, God! Floods of utter misery would overtake her without warning, forcing blinding tears down her cheeks—in the office, at home . . . She could only hope that once that date, that Red Letter Date, July the fifteenth, had passed, her emotions would return to a more even keel and she could begin to forget.

July the fifteenth duly came and went and Cressida did

at last feel she could breathe freely. There were mention in the Press as her contacts had promised there would be, and some photographs, but only of the Priory, exterior and interior shots she herself had instigated. No mention of the party or any of Damian's scurrilous pictures. She could forget the whole thing now and concentrate on building up her life again. Even the memory of Piers would fade eventually . . .

Cressida got a new job in the next town, working for a small advertising agency, and the new challenge was exactly what she needed: a complete change of environment, people and ideas which occupied her thoughts and energies almost totally.

So it was with a real sense of shock that she saw the once familiar Land Rover parked outside her parents' home one evening on her return from work.

Piers! What was he doing here? Why now? Why couldn't he just leave her alone to get on with her new life? Angrily she tried to suppress all the old contradictory longings and emotions which threatened to sweep over her again and damage her new-found but still fragile peace of mind. How dared he come here now, when he'd never so much as written to her? Well, she wouldn't see him. She would wait out of sight until she heard the Land Rover's engine start up: take him away and out of her life for ever.

Cautiously she moved just inside the front gate. It was the dining-room window which looked out that way and there were no signs of life there. She felt her heart begin pumping violently as she hurried down the path which ran along the boundary fence to the bottom of the garden. She looked back over her shoulder—no one there, no voices calling her back.

There was an old summer-house hidden away behind some shrubs, disused now and dilapidated, but it had always been Cressida's special private place for as long as she could remember. Now, if ever, she needed the sanctuary it still offered her. The door was half-open—her father must have been tidying it up. She pushed it open gently.

'Cressida . . .?'

All the breath seemed to leave her body and the colour fled her cheeks as her legs gave way beneath her. She almost fell across the threshold, but with one stride Piers was there beside her, his strong arms supporting her.

'I didn't mean to frighten you,' he said softly, 'but your mother told me you'd probably come down here when you saw the Land Rover. I guessed you might not want to see me.'

His tone changed to one of bitterness, and Cressida had to force herself not to fling her arms round him and tell him everything was all right, that she quite understood and all could be forgiven and forgotten.

But it was not as easy as that. The memories of the hurt he had inflicted on her could not be suppressed with a few soft words. She eased herself out of his embrace and stood against the wall, putting at least a few feet of space between them as a symbol of all that had changed their relationship.

'So why are you here?'

Piers flinched visibly at the coolness of her response, but his grey eyes were steady as they met hers.

'To try to make amends . . . to explain . . .'

Cressida noticed with a pang the little tattoo his fingers were beating on the old wooden table where she'd used to picnic with her dolls. She said nothing, but waited for him to go on.

'I should have come before, I know . . . you must have felt terribly hurt . . .'

Cressida bowed her head. She couldn't deny it.

'A letter wouldn't have done—I had to see you, but I had to wait till everything was settled. And then there was the Priory, the opening—you know.'

Cressida couldn't repress her curiosity.

'Did it go well—is it a success?'

'All according to plan . . . *your* plan.' There was a pause.

'And Miriam?' Cressida asked faintly.

'Miriam.' Piers' face took on a grim expression and his eyes became cold as marble as he turned away and stared out of the window. 'When you ran away, I just didn't know what to think. I couldn't really believe you had anything to do with that . . . that *orgy*——' he spat the word out, 'but then . . .'

'Miriam told you what to think,' Cressida prompted him bitterly.

'Not exactly—she was more subtle than that. She hinted, so persuasively——' Piers looked at her with a mixture of helplessness and self-loathing. 'How could I have been taken in so easily?' He took a deep breath and forced himself to continue. 'She suggested that you were really very inexperienced, perhaps not even completely reliable nor to be trusted with such a heavy responsibility. What I needed to run the Priory was someone who knew the people who mattered——'

'Like her!'

'Like her, of course,' Piers acknowledged. 'She wanted your job from the start. She had always felt she should have inherited the Priory after Hugo's death, and if she couldn't own it, being the administrator was the next best thing—a bit infra dig, but with me away so much she could slip back into her accustomed position of mistress of Clarewood Priory with no trouble at all.'

He beat his fists in suppressed rage against the edge of the table. 'I knew all that, and yet I was too blind to foresee or prevent her using her blackmailing machinations to get at me through you. But I should have seen—I have no excuse . . .' His voice trailed away in utter wretchedness.

Cressida steeled herself to go over the events of that last evening again.

'She told me if I didn't posc in that dress—which she found and made me wear . . . it wasn't my idea, honestly——'

'I know.' Piers' voice was gentle with concern, but he had to let her tell her own version of what had happened, whatever the cost to them both.

'If I didn't wear it and let that Damian take pictures of me in it, she would tell you the whole idea for the party was mine and mine alone. My first thought was to run away until it was all over, but in spite of what Miriam told you . . .' she managed a rueful smile '. . . I did take my responsibilities seriously, and I knew I had to stay around to keep an eye on what was going on. Though what I could have done if things got really out of control, I can't imagine.'

'My poor Cressida.' The tenderness with which he spoke her name made Cressida's heart lurch painfully, but there was still more to be explained.

'But you believed her,' Cressida reminded him flatly. 'You did have doubts. About me. You did think I was capable of doing something I knew you would hate *and* throwing myself at any lecherous old man who felt like making a pass at me . . . and after that last night together. Oh, Piers, you should have known me better than that.'

Her voice trembled as she stared miserably at him. He didn't attempt to deny her accusations.

'That was in the heat of the moment—oh, I know it's no excuse, and I don't expect you to forgive me, but if only you knew how much I regretted those words. As for the rest, I couldn't really bring myself to believe Miriam, in spite of her persuasive words, and she knew it. As soon as she saw me wavering, she produced the photographs.'

'Damian's—me in the dress, and with that Harry?' Cressida began to feel sick, paling at the mere memory.

Piers nodded. 'It was then I knew for sure.'

'Knew what?' Cressida's voice was scarcely more than a whisper.

'That the whole of Miriam's story was a pack of lies and a wicked fabrication. She finally overreached herself when she tried to suggest that the photos proved her point—that you were totally irresponsible and only out for a good time and what you could get out of your position at the Priory. But it was the expression in your eyes . . .'

In a sudden outburst of the rage he had been holding back all this time, Piers brought his fist down hard on the old wooden table, making dust fly up and hover in the shaft of evening sunlight filtering through the dusty window.

'Unhappy, apprehensive eyes—it stood out a mile that the girl caught in those sensuous attitudes wasn't posing willingly. And Miriam knew I had seen it, so she altered tack. If I didn't let her take your job, she would see that the pictures were in all the tabloids on opening day. She had contacts, she said. I was in a cleft stick and she knew it. I couldn't let her publish them—I had to protect you, whatever happened.'

Cressida's legs shook and she leant forward to clutch the table for support. Piers' hand reached out to her, then fell back to his side. He still hadn't finished.

'It was then that I saw red—literally.' His face lightened into a boyish grin of pure delight at the memory. 'I don't know why I'd never tried it before. I'd always prided myself on my restraint in my dealings with Miriam—not wanting to lower myself to her level, I suppose.' He shrugged. 'But this time the rage just exploded—and it was marvellous! Really liberating . . . and it had a devastating effect. I don't know that I'd ever seen a jaw drop before . . .' He paused, gloating at the memory.

'I think,' he went on slowly, as though savouring every detail, 'I told her it had been one thing leading poor old Hugo astray, bankrupting the estate in her desire to satisfy her greed, but when her malice spilled over and threatened someone I love——'

'Love . . .?' Cressida's head spun, and this time when she found Piers' arms outstretched to support her, she fell into them with a cry of joy. 'Did you say "love"?'

Piers' fingers gently caressed her cheek before moving to cup her chin as he tilted her face to his. Her eyes dwelt hungrily on every line of the features which she had never thought to see again—the golden flecks in the sea-grey eyes, the dark brows beneath the lock of fair hair—and for answer he bent his head, brushing her mouth with his warm lips searching, questioning still while he waited in turn for her response.

A wild joy surged through her, sweeping away all memories of bitterness, all the misery she had suffered during her self-imposed exile. He loved her. This strange, self-contained man whom she had once thought so cold had lowered his defences at last and admittted his love—for her, Cressida.

She pressed herself to him with a longing born of weeks of desolation, and held him close in a desperate desire to lose herself in him. 'And I love you.'

'Oh, Cressida—my dearest, most beautiful girl . . .' A deep sigh seemed to rack his whole body, then, very gently, he took her hands tightly in his and held her away from him, his eyes resting on her face with such a yearning tenderness that Cressida thought her heart would melt inside her.

'Cressida, my dearest, I need you. I only realised how

much when I thought I'd lost you for ever. I thought I could live independently—that I didn't need other people in my life . . . but I was wrong.' His fingers tightened convulsively round hers, almost painfully. 'I don't just need you—I want you, too, so much.'

He drew in his breath sharply and the grey eyes searched her face, still keeping her at a distance, not trusting himself to move closer for fear his desire for her would overwhelm his self-control.

Cressida's pulses were racing, but she said nothing—she knew there was more he wanted to say.

'Will you have me, my lady?' His voice was hoarse with emotion. 'Will you take me, my life, my home and all my lands?'

Tears filled Cressida's eyes at the strange but infinitely moving words and at the urgency in his tone reflected on every line of his face.

She nodded slowly, not trusting her own voice, and then, at last and with a gasp of release, he took her in his arms.

A long time later, when they had come back to the real world and were wandering out into the twilight to break the news to Cressida's parents, Piers heard a quiet sigh.

'What is it, my love?'

Laughter bubbled in her voice, but the words were spoken gravely.

'I don't think it's a wife you want, Sir Piers. Just an unpaid administrator. I suppose my job is still vacant?'

Piers stopped in his tracks and for a dreadful moment Cressida thought she had gone too far once again—would she never learn? She waited, tensely, for his reply, and his tone matched the gravity of her own.

'There's one thing I've discovered over the past weeks.'

Cressida looked up at him expectantly.

'The Priory needs someone very special to run it . . .' He

paused. 'Lady Aylward, in fact.'

Cressida's stomach somersaulted to the depths of despair. He wanted Miriam to stay on—in spite of everything. He couldn't, surely, not after all they had just gone through because of her.

Piers laughed gently at her appalled expression.

'I'm sorry, my love. You have to blame yourself—frivolity doesn't come naturally to me, so I have to take every opportunity to practise. Lady Aylward, sweetheart—*you* will be Lady Aylward . . . my wife.'

The future Lady Aylward shook her head in disbelief. Events had overtaken her so fast that she hadn't taken it all in yet. Then a thought struck her.

'Those terrifying ancestors . . . do you think they will still look down at me with such disapproval? I don't think I could bear it.'

Piers folded her tenderly in his arms.

'They will be as overjoyed to welcome you back as the Priory itself—and its owner.' His lips touched her hair. 'Do you remember,' he asked softly, 'a certain afternoon by the sea?'

Cressida nodded, wonderingly.

'I never finished a certain quotation.' One hand moved to rest lightly on her breast as he held her against him. ' "Oh, Cressida! How often have I wished me thus." ' There was a long silence. 'Come, my lady. We have a lot of lost time to make up for.'

Cressida looked up into his face, its outlines blurred in the gathering darkness, and touched his eyes lightly with her fingertips, knowing the golden glints would be there, deep-hidden but kindling the flame of their love and illuminating their happiness for the rest of their lives.

Have You Ever Wondered If You Could Write A Harlequin Novel?

Here's great news—Harlequin is offering a series of cassette tapes to help you do just that. Written by Harlequin editors, these tapes give practical advice on how to make your characters—and your story—come alive. There's a tape for each contemporary romance series Harlequin publishes.

Mail order only

All sales final

TO: *Harlequin Reader Service*
Audiocassette Tape Offer
P.O. Box 1396
Buffalo, NY 14269-1396

I enclose a check/money order payable to HARLEQUIN READER SERVICE® for $9.70 ($8.95 plus 75¢ postage and handling) for EACH tape ordered for the total sum of $____________*
Please send:

- ☐ Romance and Presents
- ☐ American Romance
- ☐ Superromance
- ☐ Intrigue
- ☐ Temptation
- ☐ All five tapes ($38.80 total)

Signature______________________________
(please print clearly)
Name:______________________________
Address:______________________________
State:________________ Zip:________________

*Iowa and New York residents add appropriate sales tax.

AUDIO-H

INDULGE A LITTLE SWEEPSTAKES

OFFICIAL RULES

SWEEPSTAKES RULES AND REGULATIONS. NO PURCHASE NECESSARY.

1. NO PURCHASE NECESSARY. To enter complete the official entry form and return with the invoice in the envelope provided. Or you may enter by printing your name, complete address and your daytime phone number on a 3 x 5 piece of paper. Include with your entry the hand printed words "Indulge A Little Sweepstakes." Mail your entry to: Indulge A Little Sweepstakes, P.O. Box 1397, Buffalo, NY 14269-1397. No mechanically reproduced entries accepted. Not responsible for late, lost, misdirected mail, or printing errors.

2. Three winners, one per month (Sept. 30, 1989, October 31, 1989 and November 30, 1989), will be selected in random drawings. All entries received prior to the drawing date will be eligible for that month's prize. This sweepstakes is under the supervision of MARDEN-KANE, INC. an independent judging organization whose decisions are final and binding. Winners will be notified by telephone and may be required to execute an affidavit of eligibility and release which must be returned within 14 days, or an alternate winner will be selected.

3. Prizes: 1st Grand Prize (1) a trip for two to Disneyworld in Orlando, Florida. Trip includes round trip air transportation, hotel accommodations for seven days and six nights, plus up to $700 expense money (ARV $3,500). 2nd Grand Prize (1) a seven-night Chandris Caribbean Cruise for two includes transportation from nearest major airport, accommodations, meals plus up to $1,000 in expense money (ARV $4,300). 3rd Grand Prize (1) a ten-day Hawaiian holiday for two includes round trip air transportation for two, hotel accommodations, sightseeing, plus up to $1,200 in spending money (ARV $7,700). All trips subject to availability and must be taken as outlined on the entry form.

4. Sweepstakes open to residents of the U.S. and Canada 18 years or older except employees and the families of Torstar Corp., its affiliates, subsidiaries and Marden-Kane, Inc. and all other agencies and persons connected with conducting this sweepstakes. All Federal, State and local laws and regulations apply. Void wherever prohibited or restricted by law. Taxes, if any are the sole responsibility of the prize winners. Canadian winners will be required to answer a skill testing question. Winners consent to the use of their name, photograph and/or likeness for publicity purposes without additional compensation.

5. For a list of prize winners, send a stamped, self-addressed envelope to Indulge A Little Sweepstakes Winners, P.O. Box 701, Sayreville, NJ 08871.

DL-SWPS

INDULGE A LITTLE SWEEPSTAKES

OFFICIAL RULES

SWEEPSTAKES RULES AND REGULATIONS. NO PURCHASE NECESSARY.

1. NO PURCHASE NECESSARY. To enter complete the official entry form and return with the invoice in the envelope provided. Or you may enter by printing your name, complete address and your daytime phone number on a 3 x 5 piece of paper. Include with your entry the hand printed words "Indulge A Little Sweepstakes." Mail your entry to: Indulge A Little Sweepstakes, P.O. Box 1397, Buffalo, NY 14269-1397. No mechanically reproduced entries accepted. Not responsible for late, lost, misdirected mail, or printing errors.

2. Three winners, one per month (Sept. 30, 1989, October 31, 1989 and November 30, 1989), will be selected in random drawings. All entries received prior to the drawing date will be eligible for that month's prize. This sweepstakes is under the supervision of MARDEN-KANE, INC. an independent judging organization whose decisions are final and binding. Winners will be notified by telephone and may be required to execute an affidavit of eligibility and release which must be returned within 14 days, or an alternate winner will be selected.

3. Prizes: 1st Grand Prize (1) a trip for two to Disneyworld in Orlando, Florida. Trip includes round trip air transportation, hotel accommodations for seven days and six nights, plus up to $700 expense money (ARV $3,500). 2nd Grand Prize (1) a seven-night Chandris Caribbean Cruise for two includes transportation from nearest major airport, accommodations, meals plus up to $1,000 in expense money (ARV $4,300). 3rd Grand Prize (1) a ten-day Hawaiian holiday for two includes round trip air transportation for two, hotel accommodations, sightseeing, plus up to $1,200 in spending money (ARV $7,700). All trips subject to availability and must be taken as outlined on the entry form.

4. Sweepstakes open to residents of the U.S. and Canada 18 years or older except employees and the families of Torstar Corp., its affiliates, subsidiaries and Marden-Kane, Inc. and all other agencies and persons connected with conducting this sweepstakes. All Federal, State and local laws and regulations apply. Void wherever prohibited or restricted by law. Taxes, if any are the sole responsibility of the prize winners. Canadian winners will be required to answer a skill testing question. Winners consent to the use of their name, photograph and/or likeness for publicity purposes without additional compensation.

5. For a list of prize winners, send a stamped, self-addressed envelope to Indulge A Little Sweepstakes Winners, P.O. Box 701, Sayreville, NJ 08871.

© 1989 HARLEQUIN ENTERPRISES LTD.

DL-SWPS

INDULGE A LITTLE—WIN A LOT!

Summer of '89 Subscribers-Only Sweepstakes

OFFICIAL ENTRY FORM

This entry must be received by: Sept. 30, 1989
This month's winner will be notified by: October 7, 1989
Trip must be taken between: Nov. 7, 1989–Nov. 7, 1990

YES, I want to win the Walt Disney World® vacation for two! I understand the prize includes round-trip airfare, first-class hotel, and a daily allowance as revealed on the "Wallet" scratch-off card.

Name ______________________________

Address ______________________________

City ____________ State/Prov. ______ Zip/Postal Code ______

Daytime phone number ______________________
Area code

Return entries with invoice in envelope provided. Each book in this shipment has two entry coupons — and the more coupons you enter, the better your chances of winning!

DINDL-1

INDULGE A LITTLE—WIN A LOT!

Summer of '89 Subscribers-Only Sweepstakes

OFFICIAL ENTRY FORM

This entry must be received by: Sept. 30, 1989
This month's winner will be notified by: October 7, 1989
Trip must be taken between: Nov. 7, 1989–Nov. 7, 1990

YES, I want to win the Walt Disney World® vacation for two! I understand the prize includes round-trip airfare, first-class hotel, and a daily allowance as revealed on the "Wallet" scratch-off card.

Name ______________________________

Address ______________________________

City ____________ State/Prov. ______ Zip/Postal Code ______

Daytime phone number ______________________
Area code

Return entries with invoice in envelope provided. Each book in this shipment has two entry coupons — and the more coupons you enter, the better your chances of winning!

© 1989 HARLEQUIN ENTERPRISES LTD.

DINDL-1